natural, in the two later editions, the fourth and the fifth. Some excisions did occur, and in some instances, the language of some of the more strident pronouncements of the early editions was softened.

A critical look at the text was clearly not the role of the translator here. It would, however, be interesting to see what light a future critical edition might shed on two puzzling changes observed in the fifth edition alone. The first of these occurs in Chapter III, where the fifth edition (quoted here in translation) reads as follows: "Each child now possessed a small library. Virginia and Wolfred barely cut a few of the pages." (see p. 37), whereas all earlier editions read: "Chaque enfant possédait maintenant sa petite bibliothèque. Virginia et Wolfred *faisaient leurs délices de ces nouveaux volumes, pendant que Nellie et William* en découpaient à peine quelques pages." (emphasis mine). Likewise, in Chapter IV, a passage rendered in translation, in keeping with the text of the fifth edition, as: "Old Fletcher flung aside all restraint; he became abusive; all the old clichés about Francoph*one* fanaticism came out." (see p. 65), reads in all earlier editions: "Le vieux Fletcher ne gardait plus même de mesure; il en était aux outrages; et tous les vieux clichés du fanatisme francoph*obe* y passaient:. . ." (emphasis again mine). These two textual deviations are singled out here because they raise in the mind of the present writer, rather than textual amendments explicitly decided upon by the author, the possibility of undetected printing errors which, yet, have important semantic implications.

It is appropriate to end this introduction by expressing thanks to Professor Kathleen O'Donnell for assistance in the initial stages of this project.

MICHEL GAULIN
Carleton University
July 1985

D0201660

END-NOTES

1. Most of my information concerning Groulx's life and career comes from his memoirs, published as *Mes Mémoires*, 4 vols. (Montréal: Fides, 1970-74). Henceforth referred to as *Memoirs*, followed by volume number and page. On his move into abbé Perrier's rectory, and its significance, see I, 275-281.

2. For a study of *L'Action française* and its achievement, see Susan Mann Trofimenkoff, *Action Française: French Canadian nationalism in the twenties* (Toronto and Buffalo: University of Toronto Press, 1975).

3. See *Memoirs*, II, 11-15.

4. See *L'Action française,* vol. V, no. 1, pp. 24-33. Reprinted in Groulx's *Dix ans d'Action française* (Montréal: Bibliothèque de l'Action française, 1926, pp. 123-135).

5. See *Memoirs*, II, 86.

6. *Ibid.,* III, 210-215.

7. See *Memoirs,* I, 368-370.

8. Changed to ten in the fifth (1956) edition. See "A Note on the Text", *infra*.

9. See *L'Action française*, vol. VIII, no. 1, p. 56.

10. *Ibid.,* vol. VIII, no. 2, p. 128.

11. *Ibid.,* vol. VIII, no. 3 (erroneously dated August), p. 187.

12. *Ibid.,* vol. VIII, no. 4, p. 253.

13. G. Simard, "Un Epaulement moral", *L'Action française,* vol. VIII, no. 4, pp. 210-215.

14. R. du Roure, " 'L'Appel de la race', Critique littéraire", *La Revue moderne*, vol. IV, no. 2, pp. 8-9.

15. L. de Montigny, "Un Mauvais Livre", *La Revue moderne,* vol. IV, no. 3, pp. 8-10.

16. See *Memoirs*, II, 88.

17. See, for example, *L'Action française*, December 1922, vol. VIII, no. 6 (erroneously labelled IX, no. 5).

18. J.-M.-R. Villeneuve, "L'Appel de la race et la théologie du Père Fabien", *L'Action française,* vol. IX, no. 2 (erroneously labelled 7), pp. 82-103.

19. C. Roy, "L'Appel de la race : Un roman canadien", *Le Canada français,* vol. IX, no. 4, pp. 300-315. Reprinted in his *A l'Ombre des érables : Hommes et livres* (Québec: Imprimerie de L'Action sociale, 1924), pp. 273-296.

20. "L'Appel de la race et la génération de 1880-90", *L'Action française,* vol. IX, no. 2, pp. 121-123.

21. C. Roy, "Le Patriotisme de nos vieux maîtres", *Le Canada français*, vol. X, no. 3, pp. 179-188. Reprinted in *A l'Ombre des érables,* pp. 297-311.

22. A. Maheux, "Nos Maîtres furent-ils patriotes?", *Le Canada français*, vol. X, no. 3, pp. 194-209.

23. *L'Action française,* vol. IX, no. 3, pp. 172-179.

24. *Ibid.,* vol. IX, no. 5, pp. 291-294.

25. O. Asselin, *L'Oeuvre de l'abbé Groulx* (Montréal: Bibliothèque de l'Action française, 1923). Reprinted in J. Ethier-Blais, *Discours de réception à l'Académie canadienne-française, suivi de l'Oeuvre de l'abbé Groulx* (Montréal: Hurtubise HMH, 1973).

26. For a good account of the conflict, see, among others, Robert Choquette, *Language and Religion: A History of English-French Conflict in Ontario* (Ottawa: University of Ottawa Press, 1975), particularly Part III, pp. 161-247.

THE IRON WEDGE

L'APPEL DE LA RACE

To my father and my mother
and to all the lineage of good labourers
my ancestors who, by their
great and simple life,
taught me the truth about
the greatness of our people.

[I]

For the third or fourth time, Father Fabien reread the following note, which made him intensely curious:

My dear Father,

Keep at least an hour aside for me. I need to talk to you at length. I have a double confession to make. Something serious is taking place in my life. I shall be over tomorrow, at five thirty.

Jules de Lantagnac.

Saint-Michel de Vaudreuil,
30 June 1915.

Father Fabien placed the note on his table and started pacing his room again. "Would it be the conversion this time?" he wondered. "If this really were God's will, what a leader this great lawyer might become!"

The priest was a good judge of men. Father Fabien, an Oblate of Mary, was himself a fine specimen of a man. He was tall, with square shoulders; he was of robust and well-proportioned build. His whole person was expressive of elegance, but particularly of energy. From the collar of his

1

cassock emerged a handsome head framed by thick black hair, a powerful, square-shaped head, in which the strong gentle eyes, when they stopped moving under their arch, quickly assumed a fixed look which was metallic, cold, and disconcerting. From the lips, firm but readily mobile, could come a subtle smile and a clean-sounding laugh. One sensed especially in Father Fabien spiritual health and a strongly disciplined temperament. He had a cultured mind, and was a man of doctrine and still more of prayer; the long copper crucifix inserted in his cincture represented more, in his case, than a detail of costume: it was the seal of a character and of a vocation. The highest ranking personalities of the Canadian capital asked the advice of this incomparable director of souls. Moreover, he followed closely the evolution of ideas and politics in his country. Could he not see from the window of the Oblates' house in Hull, over on the other bank of the Ottawa river, Parliament Hill, standing like an enduring horizon? Recently, circumstances had involved the Oblate very actively in the Ontario school conflict. A former professor at the University of Ottawa, he had left his heart on the adjoining soil, with his oppressed compatriots. He was continually seeking to raise up defenders and leaders for them. The word "leader" was the one that his inveterate optimism had put spontaneously into his mind just now, when he was reading Lantagnac's note.

The Oblate went back to his table and sat down. "Five o'clock," he said; "in half an hour, Jules de Lantagnac will be here."

He looked back in his mind over the history of his relationship with the man who had just announced his coming. Jules de Lantagnac had been visiting the Oblate for two years. He had come the first time for an Easter confession. From that day a frank, total friendship had developed between the two men. The lawyer was very open, and hid nothing from his confessor. For some months the latter had been able to follow the stages of a fascinating evolution in his penitent's soul.

Jules de Lantagnac was descended from an old Canadian noble family whose members had become commoners. His ancestor, Gaspard-Adhémar de Lantagnac, the first and only one of that name who had come to Canada, belonged to the military gentry. He was promoted to the rank of major of the Montreal troops in 1748, then made a knight of the Order of Saint-Louis, and became King's lieutenant in the same city. By his marriage in Québec to Mademoiselle de Lino, Gaspard-Adhémar had had thirteen children. One of his sons, Pierre-Gaspard-Antoine, Jules's grandfather, attained the rank of ensign in the troops of Louisiana. At that time, Pierre-Gaspard's kinship with the governor of New France made it possible for him to obtain a land grant, in the form of a fief in the second concession of the seigneury of Vaudreuil. Too poor to take his family to Louisiana, the ensign established them on this land. He soon had to make over, then sell a good portion of this paltry estate in order to weather the last years of the war of the Conquest. Then, one day, mystery enshrouded the ensign of Louisiana. He had already been taken prisoner, in 1746, by the Cherokees of the neighbourhood of Mobile, and for nine years had given no sign of life. From 1765 on, there was absolute silence about him. Left alone with six children, his widow struggled in vain against the already heavy burden of poverty. In a short time the descendants of Pierre-Gaspard-Antoine, who were settled by the bay of Saint-Michel de Vaudreuil, were absorbed into the peasantry. The nobiliary particle in their name was lost. From the second generation they were known purely and simply as the Lantagnacs. As years passed, by some strange mystery of popular morphology, Lantagnac was transformed into Lamontagne. By the beginning of the nineteenth century, for the worthy folk of Saint-Michel, only Lamontagnes were to be found on the second lot of the Chenaux concession.

It was there, in 1871, that Jules Lamontagne was born. He

would restore the spelling of his name only much later. For a long time the Lamontagnes remained poor. Jules was the first one that the family ventured to send to college. He was ten years old when he set off for the Séminaire de X... Gifted with a precocious but sound intellect, the boy received a solid education. One thing only was terribly lacking: education in patriotism. This, alas! was the result of the atmosphere that then prevailed in the province of Quebec.

For the historian of the future, there shall be no mystery more disturbing than the period of lethargy through which the French Canadians lived during the last thirty years of the nineteenth century. One can discern here the rapid and fatal influence of a doctrine on a people, even though that doctrine, in order to prevail, had to break down the most vigorous atavistic instincts. How indeed had it been possible for the combative vigilance of the simple folk of Quebec, which had been sharpened by two centuries of struggle, to change suddenly into a morbid liking for tranquillity? A few speeches, a few palavers from politicians had been enough. To bring their plan of federation to a successful conclusion, the men of 1867 had presented the federative pact as a panacea for all national ills. As party men, determined to carry through a party project at any cost, they made use and misuse of every argument. The false security developed and disseminated by these imprudent speeches rapidly produced a generation of pacifists. A strange state of mind immediately became apparent. It was as if all the springs of the national spirit, all the sinews of the national conscience, had suddenly slackened; or as if a knight too long encumbered with helm and breastplate had relaxed, once his armour was undone, and succumbed to sleep. Less than a quarter of a century of federalism accepted in superstitious good faith had reduced French Quebec to the most depressing listlessness. Moreover, the politicians had become the supreme guides; the demands of party alliances and the ambition to win over the English majority led them to abandon their traditional positions. Gradually the old French patriotism of Quebec weakened, with no sign of a form of Canadian patriotism growing in its place. The men of 1867 had handled and moulded the clay; they had tried to bring closer together the members of a vast body, leaving it to their successors to joint them and give them a true organic life. Unfortunately, the effort exceeded the capacity of these puny men, devoid of creative inspiration. In the long run, with the decline of parliamentary customs, what was at first only officious verbiage became a feeling, then a doctrine. Storms rumbled around 1885, with the Riel affair, and around 1890, with the Manitoba school question. The sleeping figure gave a few yawns. But the same opiates were still at work. And how could one hope that popular consciousness would suddenly spring awake, when the leaders elevated sleep to the status of a political necessity?

Such was the poisoned atmosphere in which the generation of young Lamontagne had grown up. One day Father Fabien had said to him with a sigh:

"What a strange mystery, my friend, those aberrations of the patriotic instinct among the young people of your time!"

On that day Lantagnac had replied in a slightly offended tone:

"Father, you forget one thing: I left college around 1890. What did I hear as a young schoolboy, then as a student, during Saint-Jean-Baptiste day celebrations? Query the young people of my generation about it. Ask them what sentiments and what patriotic ideas puffed out the ringing harangues we heard! The beauty, the love of Canada? The nobleness of our race, the pride of our history, the military and political glory of our forefathers, the grandeur of our destiny, do you suppose? Not at all; much more likely the advantages of British institutions, Anglo-Saxon open-handedness, the loyalty of our fathers to the Crown of England. The last item in particular, our highest, our first national virtue. As for rational, objective patriotism, based on the land and on history, a luminous conviction, a living force, that was something unknown,'' the lawyer had continued . . . ''The motherland! a hackneyed theme, an utterance that we gave voice to on such evenings, and that went the same way as the others . . . Ah! surely allowances can be made for us!'' Lantagnac had finally entreated. ''People don't have the right to forget what sad times our youth passed through. Do they know that in the context of that period the state of mind, the attitude of perpetual resignation appropriate to the conquered was almost preached to us as a duty? That to dare to dream of independence for Canada, to dare merely to speak of the union of French Canadians for political or economic defence, was represented to us as an immoral ambition? Is this known, Father?''

Lantagnac was right. When he left college, chance and the need to earn a living had led him to the office of the famous English lawyer George Blackwell. This circumstance gave him the opportunity to study law at McGill. In this environment the young man lost the last remnants of his French patriotism. In a short while he convinced himself that superiority lay on the side of wealth and numbers; he forgot French culture and the Latin ideal; he took on the arrogance that went with Anglicization. Scorn for his compatriots had not entered his heart; but pity, a lofty pity for the pauper who does not wish to be cured of his poverty. Feeling ill at ease amongst his own people, once he had become a lawyer he went to Ottawa. Thanks to his fine intelligence, his zest for work, and his talent as a speaker, he rapidly acquired an opulent clientele. Lantagnac — from then on he called himself solely M. de Lantagnac — became the busiest lawyer in the capital, and counsel to several large English companies and business houses, among them the famous construction firm of Aitkens Brothers. In the meantime he had married a young English-woman who had been converted. Four children had been born to him of this marriage: two boys and two girls. The boys had studied at Loyola College in Montreal; the younger one was still there; the girls were going to Loretto Abbey.

All went well for this Anglicized French Canadian until the day when the desire to assume some rôle awoke in him. He was then reaching his forty-third year. Wealth and good reputation at the bar were no longer enough for his ambition or for his aspirations as a person of standing. He wanted to devote himself to something greater, to broaden his mind and his existence. Being of too high-principled a nature to approach politics without preparation, he started to study again. Convinced that in Canadian politics superiority belonged only to one who had mastered the two official languages, he decided to relearn his mother tongue. Consequently he chose his authorities in political economy from among French writers. He read Frédéric Le Play, Abbé de Tourville, La Tour du Pin, Charles Périn, Charles Gide, Charles Antoine, Comte Albert de Mun, and others. There the first shock awaited him. The reading of these works was like a dazzling revelation. He was renewing contact with an order, a clarity, a spiritual distinction which delighted him. At that moment a man entered his life who was to exercise a far-reaching effect on it: it was then that Lantagnac began to visit Father Fabien. For some time, moreover, a strange, vague uneasiness, some ill-defined nostalgia for a past that he believed dead, had been stirring his very soul. Could he be the sport of a mere illusion? He felt that with the disappearance of his love for his people a corner of his heart was as empty as a desert. It seemed to him that his whole mind was out of joint, that his Anglo-Saxon mystique was dissolving like some hollow ideology. At the same time, he discovered that Protestant ideas had penetrated him to a frightening extent. This Catholic, whose conscience was pure, felt his most sacred principles being shaken every day by mysterious attacks from within. Where were these new disturbances leading him? Some spirit of free inquiry seemed to be prompting him to set up his own rules of conduct. It was an attack on his moral being that worried and sickened him.

Father Fabien was quick to diagnose the state of mind of his new penitent. "Again the iron wedge," he said to himself. From his first interviews with the great lawyer, the priest was convinced of it: a basic quality would save Lantagnac, if he could be saved: his honesty of mind, a fundamental honesty which assumed in him the form of a proud, uncompromising virtue. The young student had made his former repudiation with complete sincerity. In good faith, he had persuaded himself that for French Canadians of his type wealth and Anglicization were synonymous.

"Behind this mirage, let us open the way to the truth," reflected Father Fabien; "the illusion will vanish."

He turned his spiritual charge's attention towards French culture, even towards the great classics. It was René Johannet who wrote: "The French classics are of such a nature that it is never fitting to despair of a man of culture, any more than to despair of the salvation of French culture." In Lantagnac's case the intellectual tonic acted vigorously. Every fortnight, as he opened his briefcase to give back to Father Fabien the books he had borrowed, the lawyer spoke enthusiastically about his reading, and the tremendous effect it was producing on him. One day, more moved than normally, he said to the priest:

"It's strange, since I am becoming French again, I feel an harmonious vibration in my whole being; I am like a musical instrument that has just been tuned. But at other times, shall I say it? a strange nostalgia, an inexpressible sadness come over me. What's the use of hiding it from you? A half-dead being is stirring in me and asking to be allowed to live. I long for my village and the family home that I thought I had forgotten, that I haven't seen for twenty years."

"You will just have to go and see them again," Father Fabien had suggested.

Lantagnac was a little hesitant to undertake this trip. Whom would he find there to welcome him? His father and mother had died while he was studying in Montreal; all he had left in the old place were brothers and sisters. His change of name, his marriage to an Englishwoman, the completely English education given to his children, his rapid and substantial fortune, his pity for his people, everything had separated him from his family.

"What sort of welcome shall I get there?" he wondered, not without anxiety. A very natural embarrassment made him hesitant to reappear among his own people after an absence so long that it seemed to indicate forgetfulness. One day, however, unable to bear his uneasiness any longer, he decided to take the train. One evening in June 1915, a cab set him down at the white house on the second lot of the Chenaux concession, at Saint-Michel de Vaudreuil. It was from there that he had written his note to Father Fabien. And the latter was anxious to see the pilgrim back from the place of his birth, to hear the story of his trip, and, who knows? to find out perhaps what point he had reached in his spiritual evolution.

At five thirty someone knocked on the priest's door. Jules de Lantagnac entered. He was tall, with finely chiselled features and an impeccable bearing expressive of a natural elegance, a man possessing almost perfect distinction. There was nothing in him of the stiffness or the angular movements of a son of the soil. After more than a century and a half the great ancestor, the handsome King's lieutenant of the days of New France, had seemingly been reincarnated in his distant descendant. A slight baldness gave breadth to an already large forehead. The face did retain a few lines that were too hard, too frigid, the price paid for the sham soul that the man had put on; but the eyes and voice corrected this excessively stiff coldness, the first by their deep blue, by the impressive look of honesty that flashed from them, the second by a grave, soft quality, the tone of voice of an orator, which flowed warm and resonant from finely shaped lips, under a closely clipped moustache.

The lawyer appeared joyful and in good form; his brow was serene.

"Well! back from the homestead?" said Father Fabien,

when they had sat down after the first exchange of greetings.

"Yes, a week's pilgrimage," began Lantagnac. "And what a week, Father! What a week! Do you know that I have been thought of almost daily for twenty years? That these poor relations know everything about my paltry fame? And you should have seen the readiness and the wholehearted joy with which the old house welcomed me! Nothing like receiving the prodigal son. They went out of their way to make me forget that I might have been the guilty one. 'Be honest,' I said to them, 'you were no longer expecting me?' "

" 'Oh no, so long as one hasn't come, he's always expected,' " they replied.

"What did I tell you, Lantagnac? No courtesy can match the tact of the peasant, which is the true product of Christian charity. But now, great and esteemed seigneur," added the priest half teasingly, "what has become of your pity for the poor *habitant?*"

"My pity!" said the lawyer, frankly mortified, "let's speak about something else. Would you believe that I had great difficulty recognizing the farm? that amongst the Lamontagnes there are sons who have attended the agricultural school at Oka, and that throughout the parish, there are countless families with well educated offspring? . . . I really think that from now on I'll leave to others the cliché about an out-of-date, routine-ridden Quebec."

"And you saw the landscapes of your childhood?" queried Father Fabien, always eager to get to the point.

A misty look of pious emotion came into Lantagnac's eyes:

"Yes, I saw Saint-Michel again, and the Chenaux concession where the Lantagnacs have lived for five generations. And I confess right away that a sort of elation has stayed with me. What would be the use of denying it? My 'moral environment', as they say nowadays, is clearly in that direction. You will think me very romantic, dear Father; but after all, there is now in that corner of the world, beside the bay, a white house with a lilac-shaded gable, whose image, I can sense, will never again return to me without nostalgia. You know the countryside, Father?''

''Oh, I had a glimpse of it once, almost at a run, one autumn when I was there for a short mission. The pastor, a worthy man who was naturally very fond of his parish, had taken me on an outing; he had driven me to the high ground at what you call the Petite-Côte, I believe. There, pointing out the plain below, he had said: 'Look at that beautiful countryside!' It was beautiful, indeed. From a distance, from the top of those high banks which extend from Mount Rigaud to the Quinchien Falls, I viewed the plain that extends out into the beautiful lake, and which is gently enclosed by the blue line of the Deux-Montagnes. I noticed magnificent fields, decked with great elms, the true kings of the rich loamy soil. 'Glossy heifers', as Lamartine would have said, dotted the vast checkerboard of green and gold fields. Then, at the end of each lot, there was a house, sometimes white, sometimes grey or red, but always broad and squat, as befits a home buzzing with children. A few steps from the house stood the barns, large also, to which the high towers of the silos gave a slightly feudal appearance. What else shall I say, my dear pilgrim? With the life-giving quality of its flowing waters and its discreet, picturesque character, this countryside appeared to me the natural home of a robust, perceptive, well-balanced, hard-working people . . . Come, is that it?''

''Yes, that's the setting, and you describe it handsomely,'' agreed Lantagnac. ''Allow me however to bring you back to my own little corner, that of my pilgrimage, my true homeland. For you must know, Father Fabien, that in the beautiful region of Saint-Michel there is also the most beautiful spot in the world: the Chenaux concession.''

Then, in a joking tone:

''Let's say that immediately behind I put your own concession of Saint-Charles, in the Saint-Hermas countryside.

"I was waiting for you to acknowledge that!" said the priest.

"Really now," continued the lawyer: "you have only witnessed a very modest outburst of my zeal. How can I tell you the way those landscapes moved my heart, when I saw them again after so long! Rather than the bay of Saint-Michel, lying oval and calm in its enclosure of islands, 'small islands and islets' — to use the pleasing old words of our family contracts — I must admit that I preferred the shores of the lake. There, you see, are the Chenaux, the real ones, to which the estate of the Lantagnacs extends. There also, on the banks of the great basin, unfolds a local geography whose savour I must convey to you. Just imagine for a moment, Father Fabien, that I take you with me in a canoe, and we set off together to wander, and to gather up my memories of the beloved shore. This shore is the one that I walked all over as a child, on the days when we went among the elder groves to pick up driftwood, and gather raspberries and blackberries — particularly blackberries, my passion at that time —; it is the shore where we ran along the little path through the woods on summer mornings, soaked with dew to the armpits, in pursuit of the flock of sheep that had taken off for the beaches at the narrows. Can you see me smiling at those old, rediscovered things, in which I find myself again as in a face that resembles me? I name to myself, in my heart as much as with my lips, those places that still bear a distant echo of French history: Baie des Ormes, Grande-Pointe, Fer-à-Cheval, Grand-Rigolet, Petit-Rigolet. Then come Ile Cadieux and Ile-aux-Tourtres, islands which stand out like green circles along the shore, resembling two moles advancing towards the deep water; then between them Ile-du-Large, resembling a beacon with its clump of trees planted on its high rocks like signals; and, nearer the shore, Ile-aux-Pins, lower, more poetic, where the rustling of the reeds accompanies the organ-music of the great trees; and finally, the last, thick and darkly wooded, appropriately called Ile-à-Thomas, because at one time — an interesting little detail that I hope you'll appreciate — an old man, a certain Thomas Dubreuil, used to gather firewood there with the permission of the seigneurs, my forbears.

"Just imagine, Father Fabien," the pilgrim went on, half laughing, half serious, with a lilt in his voice, and uttering his words with a smiling emphasis, "just imagine that I have set off through the fields, and that I revisit this landscape at the end of June, a matchless period of the year in our Quebec countryside. It is the time at which the great rejuvenation of plant life and the start of maturity overlap. The trees display their rich green foliage, thick, vigorous, swollen with sap. Not a blade of grass has yet been mown. The fields of millet and clover are charged with fragrant scents; everywhere in the cherry-trees, along the fences, are nests of twittering birds. From the banks of the ditches rises the perfume of wild strawberries. Your nostrils dilate in the intoxicating air; an indefinable surge of youth and springtime flows into you, makes you throw out your chest, gives springiness to your legs, as you press forward bare-headed into the warm wind, and your feet, your poor feet sore from the hard cobblestones of the cities, almost dance on the soft grass."

Of country stock himself, Father Fabien listened to this speech, visibly affected by an emotion that recalled to him his whole rural childhood. He was careful however not to forget his urgent preoccupation:

"But, my dear poet, did these landscapes impart only memories to you?"

Lantagnac appeared hesitant. His brow suddenly clouded; the pilgrim appeared to be collecting his thoughts from afar:

"Father, you are a son of the soil like me. So you must at one time or other have indulged in pleasant evening reveries, at the far end of some field? Let's say it is the hour when the evening dew heightens the scent of new-mown hay; the eager music of the mills dies away; the countryside awaits in awed stillness the sound of the angelus . . . It is the time and place for fruitful meditations, as you remember. Almost every day, when six o'clock came, I set out, I went and sat on the back fence, beyond the last right-angled furrow, as I did as a child. I never tired of contemplating the long stretches of ploughed land and green vegetation. Before me I had the battlefield of my forbears, the old settlers, the conquerors of the virgin forests. An unremitting, fierce endeavour that absorbed the lives of five generations. And yet by what marvel has this people, in spite of a life so arduous, remained so serene of countenance and so joyful of spirit? Indeed, each time my eyes looked back over the long sections of land, they never failed to alight on a house that radiated happiness, with a wreath of thick blue smoke hovering over it, as in bygone days. A suggestive picture, and what a flow of thought it started! . . ."

"And the belfry, I am sure you didn't forget it?"

"No, my eyes turned towards the belfry. For my countrymen, it is the true centre that draws us all. And since you are longing to know, Father Fabien, I have returned in great happiness, bearing a luminous truth."

His voice took on a lyrical tone:

"No, it was not the reflection of my soul on the world. I saw that truth, I felt it everywhere: in the clear laughter of the women and young maidens, in the songs that the children sang in the evenings as they led back their cows, in the greetings that the farmers gave me by the roadside; I perceived it in their eyes when they returned from Mass on Sunday. Shall I add that in that harmony the sound of the bells appeared to me a note scarcely more dominant than the others?"

The pilgrim stopped, only to conclude with a joyous, supreme conviction:

"Everywhere, I assure you, Father Fabien, I discovered the soul of a finely tempered people, full of feeling, well-ordered in its essence, and inspired from above."

Father Fabien said approvingly:

"I was quite sure, Lantagnac, that that would be your conclusion."

Then, moving aside some of the books on his table, as if to check a protest that he felt was directed towards him, the priest went on:

"If only people could appreciate our way of life and the scenery of our countryside! But they do not; they don't know how to, or they do so with eyes that are inattentive, or coloured by visions from abroad."

Lantagnac had turned more pensive and more serious.

"Is there anything else, my dear pilgrim?" asked the priest.

"Yes, there is something else," Lantagnac began, in a restrained voice. "I extended my pilgrimage to the cemetery."

"Go on, I can picture the way there."

"You remember the cemetery at Saint-Michel. It is an old, a very old cemetery, the first and the only one in the parish. In the grass, one sees old monuments made of oak, eroded and disintegrated by time, with not a single letter of their epitaphs left. Some of them — a moving sight — are almost leaning up against the walls of the church. Here is another picturesque detail: along beside the cemetery, the Petite-Rivière flows between two rows of trees. It is given a strangely romantic air by the ruins of two manor-houses, those of my own people, which still not long ago stood on those banks. It was in this impressive setting, at a little distance from ancient feudal ruins, that a man in exile for twenty years rediscovered his forbears, and entered once again into communion with them. I can tell you, Father, that it was on the graves of my ancestors that the development of my thinking was completed; in the old cemetery I recovered my soul, the soul of a Frenchman."

Lantagnac had uttered these last words with a solemnity charged with emotion, which choked his voice. He went on, in a firmer tone:

"Thanks to you, Father Fabien, the great masters of French thought had gradually attuned my thinking; the countryside of

Saint-Michel, the people, the things, the horizon, the memories of the home in which I was born have attuned my feelings. On the graves of the Lantagnacs I attuned myself to my ancestors and my people. It was something I could feel and touch, like a palpable reality: the Lantagnac that I was earlier was going to become a chaotic, spent force. Despite myself, as I walked from one grave to the other, these thoughts assailed me: we have meaning on this earth only in terms of a tradition and a continuity. Each generation must lend support to the next. No great work of art is achieved by disjointed phrases or fragments; no great people can be formed unless its families become bound together. The voices of my dead ancestors spoke to me thus: 'It is because formerly, on the second lot of the Chenaux concession at Saint-Michel, Gailhard de Lantagnac succeeded Roland de Lantagnac, Salaberry de Lantagnac then succeeded Roland de Lantagnac *dit* Lamontagne, and Guillaume Lamontagne finally succeeded Paul Lamontagne, it is through all those, and the accumulated toil of those generations, that a portion of the motherland has been cleared, that skill in working the soil has been acquired, that great numbers of Lamontagnes have taken possession of a large part of the parish of Saint-Michel, and that in their homes has been preserved a moral strength which has unified your being once more.' ''

The priest's face showed increasing joy:

''You speak wise words, my friend.''

Lantagnac rose. His hands rested lightly on his hips, his chest was thrust proudly forward, there was an unconstrained air about his whole person; it was the stance of the orator expressing powerful emotions:

''That is not all, Father; there, in the cemetery of Saint-Michel, on the graves of my family, I made a solemn resolution. Shall I tell you what it is?''

''Go on,'' Father Fabien hastened to reply, hoping to hear from his charge the decisive word.

"I promised my ancestors that my children should be brought back and restored to them."

"Bravo!"

"My sons and daughters," continued Lantagnac, "have, through their mother, English blood in their veins; but from me they have received the venerable blood of the Lantagnacs, first those of Canada, then those of France, the Lantagnacs of Monteil and Grignan. Forty generations! I have sworn it: it is in that direction that they shall turn."

"Bravo!" repeated Father Fabien.

"I want to add that the Christian future of my children concerns me more than anything else. My recent studies have showed me above all the deep-rooted affinities between the French race and Catholicism. No doubt that is why it is called the race with a sense of the universal. Rivarol wrote of the French language that it has 'an integrity inseparable from its genius.' For myself I would add that the integrity comes to it from the best elements of Latin and Christian thought. So I have decided: my children shall be diverted from their early education. If they are willing, I shall restore them to the tradition of their forbears."

Father Fabien was exultant. He rose in his turn; he took the hands of his spiritual charge and pressed them affectionately:

"Ah, my friend, thanks be to God! At last you have come to it! If you only knew how long I have been waiting for you! Lantagnac, I am going to use a word that will perhaps surprise you: today is a great day for the French minority of Ontario: a leader is born to them!"

For a moment the two men looked at each other without speaking, stirred to their innermost depths. Lantagnac was the first to break the silence:

"Father, I beg of you, spare my weakness. I haven't the right to forget that I am still only a neophyte."

"Not so," Father Fabien interjected, "a convert, which is quite another thing."

"But will the convert persevere?" insisted Lantagnac; his humility was sincere. "Shall I manage to free myself entirely? If you only knew how weak I feel as I face the return to my old milieu, inwardly a different person. And then, between my children and me there is someone . . . Alas, I know only too well that in taking them away from their English upbringing, I shall be taking them away from their mother. Can I do it without preparing the way for a catastrophe?"

Father Fabien used his best efforts to comfort the convert:

"Have no fear, my friend. An aristocrat like you is a diplomat from birth; you will overcome the external obstacle. You have heard the call of something irresistible. There is more. The iron wedge has entered into you; it will complete its work, despite you if necessary."

And as the lawyer appeared to be waiting for an explanation, the Oblate went on:

"Have you ever asked yourself, Lantagnac, why there are these conversions, these total reversals of direction as you are experiencing, that occur round the age of forty? Here is my particular theory; I call it the theory of the iron wedge. I tell myself that the psychological and moral personality, the true one, cannot be composite, made up of ill-assorted parts. Its nature, its law is unity. For a time, foreign layers may adhere to it, even adapt to it. But an internal principle, an unshakeable force pushes a human being to become uniquely himself, as the same law requires a maple to be only a maple, an eagle to be only an eagle. Now everyone knows that this law operates more particularly when man is advancing towards what Dante calls 'the middle of the road of life.' If the man is moulded of good clay, if the underlying personality is vigorous, this is for him the unique instant, the moment of maturity when he resolves to take possession of his full strength, when he seeks to unify his thought and his moral being. Then take heed! It is also the time of the iron wedge. The least circumstance, an incident, a word, a mere nothing — a pilgrimage, for example to one's birthplace — introduces the wedge at the point where the true foundation of the person and the artificial layers are welded together. The result is rapid and sudden. The foreign layers are shattered to pieces. The personality is liberated. And the true man, the unified man rises up, emerges as the statue emerges from its matrix. Thus, my friend,'' concluded Father Fabien, ''go bravely towards the future. Deliverance is at hand.''

''Say rather: the work and the struggle are beginning,'' replied Lantagnac.

[II]

At 240 Wilbrod Street that day, concern was growing about Jules de Lantagnac's long absence. The family had just sat down for dinner; its head had not yet returned.

"Wasn't Dad supposed to be back at noon?" asked Nellie, the elder daughter.

"Yes indeed," answered Madame de Lantagnac; "his last postcard said he would return on the 11:30 train."

"I just hope he has been able to leave his gloom there," interjected Wolfred, the elder son. "Really, I think he's very tired."

"I think so too," replied Madame Lantagnac. "Don't you find that long trip a little strange, going to see a family he hasn't seen for twenty-three years, and particularly wanting to go alone?"

"That's quite natural," said Virginia, the younger girl; "our dear father is too kind-hearted to forget for ever. Then, frankly, what was the point of our going to Saint-Michel, when we don't speak their French?"

"Their French," exclaimed Nellie; "you mean their patois. Ah! can't you just see it! Dad going back to that language!"

"Anyway, let him get here as soon as possible," added William, the younger boy. "I am anxious to be off to the country. Sandy Hill's suffocating in this heat. And Dad gives us such a fine description of his beloved Quebec."

- - - - - - - - - -

20

While his family was worrying about his protracted absence, Jules de Lantagnac was only just leaving Saint-Michel. On the morning of his departure, despite his eagerness to get back home, he had set off again through the fields, for a last stroll. He wanted to condense, to soak up, as he said, his exhilarating impressions. Moreover, he had decided to go and see Father Fabien before returning home. He felt haunted by the solemn promise he had made to his ancestors in the cemetery; he burned to tell the priest the outcome of his experience. It was now seven o'clock in the evening. He was returning home repeating to himself the last words he had uttered just now, on Father Fabien's threshold: "The work and the struggle." At the moment of beginning his new life, Jules de Lantagnac felt the fear of himself, the movement of recoil that even the most steadfast know well. Once the enthusiasm of the dream has fallen, like the curtain in the theatre of old, the action and the tragedy begin. The lawyer was of too sincere a nature not to dread that grave sentence of Father Fabien still echoing in his ears: "A leader is born to us!"

As he started to cross the interprovincial bridge to return to Ottawa, the convert saw looming before him, a symbol of his stern future, the image of the capital with its steep cliffs. To the right, on the hill, were the Houses of Parliament and other buildings of the federal government; on the parliamentary tower, the conqueror's flag waved arrogantly. To the left, he could see the Mint, a squat construction like a factory, and the scarcely more elegant building that housed the Archives; further on, in the centre, stood the red brick structure of the King's Printer, and the turreted walls of the Customs Department. So many places, so many institutions, Lantagnac reflected to himself as he walked, where the French Canadians obtained only with difficulty their share of influence and employment. High on its pedestal, the English Upper Town itself, more than all the rest, seemed to flaunt the domination of the conqueror over the conquered, whose more modest districts stretched out in the direction of Lower Town. In this panorama of defeat, however, a vision suddenly caught Lantagnac's eye. In front of him, at the tip of Nepean Point, a man of bronze, of heroic stature, stood erect on his plinth, facing the town, with his foot thrust boldly forward and his astrolabe in his hand. This knight with his high, wide-topped boots, and his broad, felt hat of bygone days, is Samuel de Champlain, a hero sprung from the French race, the founder of New France.

This vision in this landscape, Champlain armed with his astrolabe, in order to trace out for his own people the path to unlimited conquest, appeared to Lantagnac a symbol that corrected the first one and fortified his courage.

"What a fine energetic race were the French of former times!" he said to himself. "They needed only an astrolabe or a compass to go to the ends of the earth."

With a lighter step he hurried towards Wilbrod Street, where he had lived for ten years, almost opposite St. Joseph's Church. As he went, he involuntarily began to consider how he should proceed.

"Presently," he reflected, "I shall return home, with a totally altered mind. I am returning to my wife and children a different, an entirely new man. None of my family knows anything about it; nobody suspects anything. Nobody must suspect. If I am to win over my children, must it not be without their knowing, especially without their mother knowing? Ah! their mother . . ."

Lantagnac felt all his worries overcoming him. "Their mother!" he repeated, still troubled, "their mother! May she not suspect in my new zeal a threatening revolution, an encompassing strategy intended to remove her children's minds from her guidance, and even to rob her of their affection? And supposing the thought, the fear of that dispossession were to upset everything between us? Supposing even that my advocacy of the French cause were to awaken and sharpen the nationalistic instinct in her?"

Lantagnac saw rising before him the kind of obstacle which one first surveys without knowing whether it can ever be overcome or brushed aside. When he had arrived in Ottawa twenty-four years before, his business connections had led the young lawyer towards the English drawing rooms of Sandy Hill.* There one day he met Maud Fletcher, the daughter of a senior official in the Department of Finance. The two young people quickly took a liking to each other. There was however an obstacle to their union: Maud belonged to the Anglican Church. More attached to his religious than to his national faith, young Lantagnac vowed to bring about his fiancée's conversion. At first the Fletchers were not very pleased about this. Fortunately for the young man, in Maud's family religious faith was now no more than a form of national faith. The religion of the *flag*,** the British and imperialist faith, reigned supreme in the thinking and feeling of these very orthodox Anglicans. For them, as for the majority of English Canadians, who are only third or fourth generation Canadians, *Old England, the Old Mother country* held the charm and dignity of the only *home,* the sole motherland. The Fletchers, once fully reassured as to the perfectly Saxonized mentality of the young suitor, dropped their resistance. Maud became a sincere convert, and Jules de Lantagnac married her. In the early days of their marriage, the young man indulged in the thrill of a victor; he proudly paraded his wife, as if she were a conquest. For him, who had turned Anglomania into a mystique, this marriage became his official affiliation to the superior race, the *populus Anglicus.* And he firmly intended that his heirs should continue the triumphant step. To which of the two spouses, to which of the two peoples would the minds of his children belong? The very names they were given at

* The French Canadians still say: *La Côte-de-Sable*. (Groulx's note)
** Italicized words or expressions in this paragraph are as in Groulx's original French. (Translator's note)

baptism indicated this unequivocally. The elder of the sons retained the trace of his double origin: he was called Wolfred-André de Lantagnac; but for the others a single first name had sufficed, an English-sounding name; they were called in order of age Nellie, Virginia and William.

Wolfred, Nellie, Virginia, William! Lantagnac murmured these names to himself; more than anything else they recalled to him the kind of atmosphere he had wanted in his home.

"And it is I," he had to agree, "who let these names be imposed on me. Imposed! What am I saying? I, rather, who welcomed them with joy, as a sign of the social assent of my name and my family! Isn't it I again who broke with the French society of the capital and let myself be drawn over completely to my wife's side? And still I who chose to speak one language only in my house, a language which is not the old language of the Lantagnacs?"

Alas! of the Anglomania of which he accused himself in humiliation, he had made himself the doctrinarian, the fervent proselyte, the enthusiastic apostle.

"How often, before my children, have I not gone into ecstasies over Anglo-Saxon superiority, over the excellence of the greatest imperial race in history, a race of governors, a race of world masters . . . One of the first books that I got my sons to read was the breviary, the handbook of Anglo-Saxon imperialism called *The Expansion of England,* by Seely! And it will be for me," he reflected with embarrassment, "to say to those same children tomorrow: 'that was all an illusion and a lie! My sons and daughters, I have led your minds astray. Superiority is of another essence.' "

As he was pondering these thoughts, Lantagnac arrived home. There was the house, spacious, middle-class in appearance, but elegant, with a wide verandah along the front. He had barely slid back the bolt of the iron gate to the front lawn when Virginia, the younger of his daughters, who was then sixteen, ran and threw herself into his arms.

"How long you have been, you naughty old Dad!" she cried, in a scolding, half-bantering tone.

"Eight days! Is that so long?" teased her father.

"Oh, the naughty one!" his daughter went on, "he's going to try and make us think he didn't find the time long, as long as we did, at least."

Glad to find himself back amongst his family, Lantagnac scarcely noticed that his wife and children spoke only English to him. During the evening meal, which was served to him in haste, everybody sat round the table and all began to talk at the same time, asking questions about the trip, the relatives at Saint-Michel, those unknown relatives that they were most eager to get to know. This Quebec world seemed so new to them, something never before revealed, a beautiful rustic scene from a film or picture from a magazine. Lantagnac had to answer ten questions at once. How many times that evening, just back from his childhood home, his heart full with the emotions of the past, and his memory enchanted with the poetic landscapes of Saint-Michel, did he not find himself obliged to parry the painful blows which all unconsciously his own children dealt him! Thus William had asked him:

"But how did you make out, Dad, as meticulous and particular as you are, sitting and eating at the table of the Lamontagnes? Those Quebec *habitants* are said to be so dirty!"

He had barely replied to William that nothing was whiter than the tablecloth of the *habitants* before Nellie returned to the assault with an even more offensive question:

"But Dad, you could talk to them then? You hadn't forgotten their patois?"

This time Lantagnac could not restrain a frank burst of laughter:

"Their patois? My poor children! You have no idea how they make fun of the *Parisian French** you are sometimes

---

* In English in Groulx's original. (Translator's note)

taught in our high schools and collegiates. Our relatives on the Chenaux concession at Saint-Michel read the papers; they even read magazines. But do you know what those papers and magazines sometimes offer their readers for comic relief? Nothing less than specimens of the *Parisian French* of Ontario! If only you could see, my poor little ones, the hilarious success that such items always enjoy in Quebec!''

No doubt about it, the children no longer understood.

''Is it true,'' Wolfred had also asked, ''that the *habitant* still farms his land as in the time of the French settlers, using the same methods and the same antiquated machinery?''

With warm feeling, Lantagnac then described to his children the paternal home, the property of the Lantagnacs, *dits* Lamontagnes, as he had just seen it, after more than twenty years. He described the house, reconstructed, but retaining many of its original parts; he described the farm buildings, entirely remodelled and updated in accordance with the most recent developments; he spoke to them of their cousins, whose diplomas as graduates of the agricultural school at Oka hung in the living room; he described the fine herd of Holstein cows; he made them see the broad stretches of rolling cultivated land, the Percheron teams at work with the most modern equipment: the automatic mower, the manure spreader, the disk harrow, the binder, etc. Finally, above the landscape, the poet sketched the profiles of the giant elms opening out their royal parasol in the golden evening light! The air was thick with enthusiasm. Immediately they all wanted to set out for Saint-Michel, to visit the worthy Lamontagnes of the Chenaux concession.

Here was Lantagnac's chance to get his own back!

''No, not now.''

''Why not?'' ventured Nellie.

''Because your relatives at Saint-Michel would not understand your patois, my poor child,'' replied her father, laughing heartily.

Everyone was amused at the rejoinder. Lantagnac, who

wanted to strike while the iron was hot, therefore suggested to them that they should have at least an hour's French conversation a day, during the entire holiday.

"Do you agree?"

A unanimous "yes" showed the future teacher that his students were favourably disposed. That same evening, as he was going into his room, someone stopped him as he passed. It was Virginia. She put an arm around her father's neck, kissed him gently, and whispered in his ear:

"I can't tell you how much I am going to like our French lessons! I've been waiting so long for them, that I was even thinking of asking you!"

These words of his younger daughter touched the father's heart. Certainly everything would go well. That evening, the convert from Saint-Michel slept, with the joy of first victory.

The next day they set off for their holidays at Lake MacGregor. Lantagnac had just bought a summer home there, some twenty miles from Ottawa and barely half a mile from the mouth of the river Blanche in the heart of Quebec. He had chosen it on an isolated, steep-sloped island, which rose out of the depths of the lake like the old crest of a buried mountain. In this restful place, the lawyer hoped to satisfy his liking both for tranquillity and for the picturesque. Above all he wanted to find new vigour, for himself and his family, in a French atmosphere. That year, having still a fortnight's holiday, he had decided to take it with his children. He had said to himself: "The opportunity is too good to miss; let's assume our rôle as teacher right away." Towards the evening of their first day on the island, the lake, which had been a bit unsettled earlier, became perfectly calm again. The idea of taking out a boat was an appealing one.

"Let's go on the lake," said the children.

"Let's go on the lake," agreed their father.

He packed all his family into a boat, which was quickly pushed out into the water; it was decided that the first French lesson should take place in the open air. Lantagnac gave the order to steer towards the far side of a bay, where the lake appeared to widen and the mountains to get higher. Suddenly the sound of a brass band made the rowers stop.

"What's that music, in this solitude?" asked Madame de Lantagnac.

"That's probably the Oblate brothers," replied her husband. "Their summer home is at this end of the lake."

"But didn't Father Fabien tell us about these outdoor concerts?" asked Nellie next.

"That's right," said her father. "And they give them, it appears, in a large boat in the middle of the lake, to have the advantage of echoes from the mountains. Listen . . ."

The band, as they approached, was playing a medley of Canadian songs. Then they noticed here and there off the islands, the brothers in canoes rowing quietly, no doubt seeking the spots in the solitude where the echoes were heard most clearly. Just opposite, from the back of a deep cove, it seemed that a mocking genie, like an incomparable mimic, was taking up the jaunty refrains one after the other: *A Saint-Malo beau port de mer . . . Derrière chez-nous y-a-t-un étang . . . En roulant ma boule . . .* and finally the languorous melody: *Perrette est bien malade . . .*

"What pretty things those airs are!" exclaimed Madame de Lantagnac, enraptured.

"They are old Quebec songs," said Wolfred; "I recognize them now. At Loyola, our French-Canadian classmates like to sing them to us."

"You should hear how nicely they sing them at Saint-Michel!" added Lantagnac, brought back to his pilgrimage by the old songs.

A fairly long interlude followed. The evening was drawing in. Away behind the hills the fire of the sun, red a few minutes earlier, was fading out like pale candlelight. Suddenly the brasses struck up, with the final piece: *O Canada, terre de nos aïeux!* The sprightly genie of the deep cove was silent. It was as if he were leaving it to the voice of the high peaks to make itself heard. As each phrase of the patriotic symphony was borne on the air, the great echoes in the distance took it up, harmonized it on their keyboard, exalted and developed it with a grandiose rhythm. Giant organs pealed in vast crescendos along the escarpments; and, in the resonance that filled the air, one might have said that the national anthem became the natural acclaim, the inner song of the Canadian soil.

The children were overwhelmed. They were not less so by the sight that greeted their eyes as they rowed slowly back towards shore. The wild nature of the Laurentians lay plainly visible, that evening, in the calm of a matchless summer night. Silence had descended upon the lake and the tall timber. One could barely make out, by listening closely, the mysterious vibration coming from the swarming life on the granite face of the high rocks. Sometimes, at rare intervals, a chorus of whip-poor-wills, or the shrill piping of the loon, rose from the recesses of the bays, only to die away immediately and intensify the silence. The boat was barely gliding over the still, dark, deep water. From time to time they passed through zones of warm air, the gentle moist breathing of the lake, which was immediately tempered by a smell of pine resin, borne from the shore on the evening dew. On the mountain side appeared a little clearing. In its centre, a small white house was sleeping with the heavy sleep that follows arduous toil. From the chimney of its grey, pointed roof, a few wisps of thin smoke escaped — the only movement — like an exhausted prayer tapering off into sleep. Meanwhile, overhead, the moon was rising in a clear sky. Under its white gleam, the mountains revealed their glistening crests, and the silvery green of their great forests. Then, by rapid gradations, this brightness diminished, and was swallowed up in the fawn tones of the slopes and the sombre gorges. The scene was both striking and impressive. The white orb, seemingly motionless, gave a religious silence to this nocturnal landscape, something of the hushed reverence of nature feeling itself to be in the presence of God.

In the boat, no one had spoken for some moments. More than the others, Lantagnac was sensitive to the solemnity of the scene. What solicitous Providence had so arranged things and events that on his children's first contact with the Quebec motherland, the latter had been revealed to them in the fullness of its charm and splendour? There was rejoicing in his heart. The wafts of warm air that sometimes caressed his brow, and came to him from the depths of great nature herself, under a divine light, seemed to him a wind of happiness, the breath of a new future in which his life would begin again on an enlarged plane. Virginia was the first to break the silence:

"What a beautiful spot the Quebec Laurentians really are!" she exclaimed, as she looked up towards the silent slopes. "Isn't there a natural inclination to speak French here?"

"Yes," said Wolfred, "it seems so natural."

And French conversation was resumed in earnest. After such an auspicious beginning, it continued on the following evenings, sometimes on the lake, but most often in the living room, or on the verandah. Each brought himself to it with a tremendous zest. Everyone wanted to take part. The atmosphere of the countryside appeared to have a beneficial effect. Madame de Lantagnac herself would come and sit near the group, with her embroidery basket, and as she worked her crochet hook she would join in the conversation, occasionally venturing timid little phrases. So well that, as the days passed, Lantagnac became convinced that his family's spirit was becoming more harmoniously attuned to that of the land.

Alas! why did the poor students, and their master even more so, soon have to sing a different tune? The whole class thought it was speaking impeccable French, but the teacher found himself faced with the kind of *beastly horrible French** which

---

* In English in Groulx's original. (Translator's note)

the Toronto papers mock so bitterly, and ascribe to the *habitants* of Quebec. Wolfred and William perhaps spoke somewhat better, having associated with French-Canadian classmates at Loyola College. Nellie and Virginia, for their part, spoke, goodness gracious! the real French of Ontario essence, pure, authentic *Parisian French*.* Not only had their father to teach them a new, unknown language; he had first to overcome the pretentious and barbaric jargon with which wrong teaching had cluttered their minds.

Meanwhile the holidays came to an end. The summer home was closed, and the family returned to Wilbrod Street. Nellie and Virginia did not go back to Loretto Abbey. Their mother had decided to keep them at home with her and entrust them to a private tutor. Maud's decision, which was quite unexpected, puzzled Lantagnac a great deal, but he did not venture to oppose it. Wolfred, who was intending to take law, instead of going to Toronto set off for the French university at Montreal, much to his father's astonishment and joy. But Wolfred, the mysterious personage who never gave away his thoughts, immediately deflated a joy which he deemed too hasty.

"Going to Montreal is only natural," he was careful to state. "I shall be with my Loyola friends; then, as I intend to practise in Ottawa, my most elementary interest commands me to become bilingual."

As for William, he had rather grudgingly agreed, at the earnest request of his father, to go to the French university in the capital. But after three weeks, the obstinate student put up such a dogged resistance to study and assignments that he had to be sent back to Loyola College.

This was a real coup de théâtre, but not the last one, in the Wilbrod Street house. Very saddened by William's lack of discipline, Lantagnac was much more perturbed by Maud's behaviour in this affair. The gravest indications gave him reason to suspect a conspiracy between mother and son. What had been going on in Maud Fletcher's mind for some time now? Her change of attitude was unmistakable. How could

Lantagnac have forgotten, for example, that unfortunate scene which had taken place on the last evening of the holidays? The family had returned that same day to the Wilbrod Street house. The French class was just about to begin. The teacher had seated himself in his armchair. That evening, the last before Wolfred's departure, he had promised himself that he would put more spirit than ever into his task, more persuasive affection, so that the impetus acquired during the holidays would continue. Suddenly Maud, who was sitting in the circle, drew attention by rising vivaciously; she quickly gathered up her knitting, her scissors, her balls of wool and thread, and went off to the far end of the living room, to work by herself. It was a painful shock to everybody. One felt that a drama was beginning to unfold. Looks were exchanged between the children: of embarrassed surprise between Wolfred and Virginia, of barely disguised complicity between Nellie and William. That evening, Nellie and William gave the lesson only distracted attention. Madame de Lantagnac never appeared again at the French class.

What was taking place in Maud Fletcher's mind? Lantagnac would soon open his eyes to the hard truth.

[III]

Barely a few days had passed since William's departure for Loyola College. Lantagnac, who no longer needed to remain in the living room after dinner now that the French classes were definitely ended, was returning to an old habit of his. Having lit his cigar, he donned a cap, put on a coat and resumed his former walks on the verandah. A long association with business had not destroyed his bent for meditation. He liked these evening walks very much. They allowed him an escape from the constricting anxieties of his Elgin Street office, the countless worries of his exhausting life. These few moments of solitude brought a relief to his brain, a pleasant diversion to a man of thought who wanted to handle things other than figures and articles of the Code. On that late September evening, Lantagnac felt more than ever the need to be alone. William's little revolt had affected him deeply. He saw it as a serious failure in his plans for his children.

"There are at least two of them, perhaps three," he said to himself, hammering out the words bitterly, "who are going to escape me. True, Wolfred has taken up French: he has even set about it with a will. But what's the good of deceiving myself? Wolfred is really only a dilettante, greedy for culture. As for Nellie, a terribly stubborn child whom her mother has completely taken control of, what can one expect of her?"

He had reached that point in his melancholy reflexions when Virginia appeared on the verandah. He had seen her through the curtains, under the half lowered blind, as she was picking up her coat and getting ready to go out. His younger daughter, as he guessed, was coming to walk with him; he felt happy about that. Recently Virginia had become a real confidante to him; with her, he knew, he could open his heart completely.

"Do you want company, Dad? I don't like seeing you alone like this," she said, scolding him affectionately. "You seem to be in the doldrums."

"You're always welcome, Virginia, you know that," he replied, offering his arm.

Then, avoiding his daughter's remark, he said:

"Well now, how is your study of French going? Tell me about it."

"Oh, very well, it couldn't be better," began Virginia right away, with the warmth and enthusiasm that marked everything she said. "Did I tell you? I don't have only one French master now, I have two. I had to find some use for the money you give me so generously for my small expenses."

And, as her father made a slight gesture of disapproval:

"Don't blame me; the other day I went to the Rideau Street Convent. One of my French-speaking friends, for I have some now, had told me: 'Go and see Sister Sainte-Anastasie; she is more than a good nun, she is a patriot who knows her language admirably well.' So I went to the convent; I saw Mother Sainte-Anastasie; and it's agreed: I shall go twice a week for a lesson. You see, Father," the young girl continued, lowering her voice slightly, "I found myself the other day in a gathering of young French-Canadian girls. Would you believe that many of them only spoke English? That upset me. I told myself that a young Lantagnac owed it to herself to do differently. Am I wrong?"

Lantagnac pressed the dear child's arm against his own. With joyous surprise, he realized that she had spoken to him, this time, in a French that was almost faultless.

"Ah! my little Virginia," he exclaimed, "you are the true daughter of your forbears. So you really love studying French?"

"I am terribly fond of it, Father; and I do learn quickly. It's strange: French comes back to me as if it were a language I had once known. Mother Sainte-Anastasie tells me that I have intuition, that I only have to look into myself to learn anything."

"Does Mother Sainte-Anastasie teach you only French?"

"She also teaches me the history of French Canada. It's I who asked her to. Would you know that I am finishing Ferland, that I've read Faillon, that I shall read Garneau as well? Oh! what beautiful books, Father! You know how I love stories of chivalry. That's where I find my finest *chansons de geste*. The Iroquois wars, the heroism of Dollard and Madeleine de Verchères, the discovery of the Mississippi and the West, the journeys of our noble men to Hudson's Bay, the deeds of our martyrs, all that is pure epic, isn't it? A great epic of chivalry, with a Christian content, in a marvellous setting! Better still, my reading revives in me, in some indefinable way, the memory of an ancient hereditary soul. Do you remember that evening when you said to me, right here: 'Virginia, it is not only four generations of Lantagnacs that call to you; there is also the long line of female forbears, those of France, then those of New France, all the heroic women who have made our family.' No, Father, that voice of our ancestors, that call from the past is no fancy. I hear it clearly within me, as I read their history . . ."

Here the young girl paused. She rested her head on her father's shoulder, and said in a tone of complete conviction:

"No, I am not mistaken. I really feel quite changed. It's just as you had told me, Dad: as I become French again, I think more clearly and feel more perceptively."

Lantagnac listened to his child, without interrupting, but just looking fondly at her whenever, at the end of the verandah, a ray of light from inside reflected on her. He considered with pride this handsome, dark-haired girl, full of fervent lyricism, a sweet and vibrant creature, whose cheeks blushed when strong feelings stirred her heart.

"So you are completely happy, my dearest?"

Suddenly, to relieve his mind of the remorse that sometimes attacked him, he ventured:

"You are not angry with me for taking you away from your early upbringing?"

"Angry with you? How could I be?" Virginia replied quickly. "As for happy, that is different . . ."

The child lowered her voice; then, concealing with difficulty a secret sorrow:

"I would be happy if it weren't for Mother . . ."

"What do you mean, Virginia?" asked Lantagnac anxiously.

"The fact is, Father, you can't have failed to notice it, the fact is that Mother has been unhappy for some time, very unhappy. If she didn't want us to go back to Loretto Abbey, it was because she felt alone, terribly alone in her own house, as she said to us."

"Alone in her own house? How's that?" said Lantagnac, coming to a stop.

"Ask Nellie; she is Mother's confidante; perhaps she'll tell you more. With me she feels terribly uneasy. She avoids me as much as possible. But I know that she often cries."

"And how long have the sadness and tears been going on?" asked Lantagnac, still more worried.

"Since we've been doing French. No doubt you know that it was she who turned William away from the University of Ottawa. One day at lunch, when I was urging him to stay with us, Mother suddenly said:

'It is your privilege, William, to continue your studies in English, as it is Virginia's right, I suppose, to take two French lessons instead of one."

"So she knew about the Rideau Street Convent?"

"No, but I had told William."

At that moment Virginia, who was beginning to get cold,

asked for permission to go in. Lantagnac continued to walk by himself. What he had just heard had deeply upset him. Truth to tell, Virginia's confidences as to Maud's state of mind were not a revelation; he partly suspected it, although he had not attached to it this degree of seriousness.

"So," he said to himself, "she did support William in his revolt; she pushed him into it; she went that far!"

On to the floor of the verandah the first autumn leaves, torn away by the wind, were slipping down one by one. They went past with the slight grating sound of crumpled paper, the flight of things faded and mournful. And Lantagnac, heartsick, wondered why, that evening, that same autumn wind filled his heart with the rustle of dead leaves. A deep disquiet came over him. Was this the end of his dream? Was it going to fail to develop?

"Perhaps," he blamed himself, "I haven't been diplomatic enough. Perhaps I should have been patient, gone more slowly, not counted so much on the enthusiasm of the early days . . ."

No, really, in his first flush of eagerness, like a man of action anxious to press on, he had scarcely cared about the stages. Whole cases of French books, he recalled, had arrived from bookstores in Montreal. Each child now possessed a small library. Virginia and Wolfred barely cut a few of the pages. To the journals and magazines in the den, he had likewise added the best journals from France and Quebec, which received the same consideration and the same lack of response as the books. How far had his convert's zeal not gone! Again in order to strengthen the new atmosphere in the home, Lantagnac had decided to substitute for the pictures and prints, all of them, alas, in the American or Anglo-Saxon style, which hung here and there in the various rooms of his house, reproductions of the best works of the French classical school. He had even interspersed with them some Canadian works. In Wolfred's room, a *Dollard sonnant la dernière charge* by Delfosse, had some time ago replaced a George

Washington in full general's dress. In Virginia's room a good copy of the *Jeanne d'Arc* by Ingres had taken the place of an indeterminate work by Reynolds. In the corridor leading to the large living room, a Louis-Hippolyte LaFontaine now occupied the gilt frame of a portrait of Lord Monck and a Louis-Joseph Papineau that of a portrait of Lord Durham.

"No doubt it was too much too quickly!" Lantagnac went on, and he continued to blame himself and confess to his guilt:

"No, no, I handled it wrongly. What did I do, in short to prepare Maud for the transition? Rather what have I not done to make it disconcerting, almost impossible for her? By breaking with my own people before my marriage, by repudiating all my relations with the French in this very place, have I not inevitably cast her back among her own kind, rendered her defenceless against the Anglo-Saxon mentality? Then, why hide it from myself? I have been happy with Miss Fletcher, but with a happiness that quickly discovered its boundaries. One can say what one likes: a difference of national background between husband and wife restricts intimacy. If souls are to blend so as to be a true reflection of each other, there must first exist between them perfect spiritual affinities, identical, congenital ways of thinking and feeling. I know it too well! Because of our differences, in a whole part of my inner life I have remained impenetrable and isolated. It has no doubt been the same with Maud. The mother in her had to comfort the wife. I relinquished to her the education of my children; she alone chose a college for my sons, a convent for my daughters. But then what was to happen did happen. Maud made it her purpose to appropriate more fully what I abandoned to her. Her children were her whole life. Can I be surprised now, if after reigning in this domain as an all-powerful mistress, and for so long, she is surprised in her turn, and even suffers because of my sudden mingling? Yes," Lantagnac went on, for the hundredth time, "yes, there is nothing in Maud's behaviour which is not both natural and inevitable. But, what if there were something else? If to the surprise and grief of being dispossessed were added, as in my case, the return of the hereditary instinct?''

It was at that point in his analysis that Lantagnac drew back abruptly. His reflections veered off in another direction because he was afraid that by embarking on this course he would end up in an abyss. His thoughts leapt on, then doubled back on themselves, as if the road, by getting longer, might lead to a different outlet.

But in spite of himself, he soon had to face the abyss, and the dizziness it brought. One evening Lantagnac was sitting alone with Maud. A good hour before, Virginia and Nellie had gone to their rooms. Conversation between the spouses flagged. Hardly an occasional word, or a remark often left unanswered, broke the monotony of the slow ticking of the big Norman clock in the corner of the living room. Each held a book; but the eyes of both were straying far beyond the pages. Lantagnac ventured to break this half-silence, which he found oppressive:

''Are you unwell, Maud, that you don't say anything?''

Maud bent her head more closely over her book. Suddenly, her breast heaved in a convulsion that had been held in too long; she broke into sobs.

Lantagnac had risen.

''But, then, what is it, my poor child?''

Maud closed her book hastily.

''The trouble is, my friend,'' she replied, her words interspersed with bursts of tears, ''the trouble is that you have regrets about your marriage and that our happiness is over.''

Lantagnac did not have time to reply. Maud ran out of the living room and up the main staircase, leaving her husband alone, confronted with the agonizing reality, which was, this time, irreversible.

The poor husband now understood, in earnest, that his life was moving towards tragedy. While he stood there, in the cold isolation of this big living room, a very clear vision crossed his mind. He perceived, in his own existence, what his experience of the courts, particularly the assize courts, had made harshly clear to him: the implacable repercussions of a mistake throughout a whole life, the fatal succession of expiations. Some lives, he knew, were ruined by a single error, thrown completely out of joint. Lantagnac could no longer doubt that he had committed this kind of mistake himself, twenty-three years previously; and here were the harsh repercussions beginning to reach him.

This scene with Maud, and the painful reflections that followed, reduced the convert's ardour considerably. At first he only felt a weariness which he resisted. But gradually, temptation and discouragement came to the fore, and invaded the whole field of his consciousness. Now that he could confront the merely probable gains from his efforts with the certain and terrible losses, was it worth risking so much? What was the good, really? Had not his more intimate contacts with his children provided sufficiently disturbing revelations?

"What was it like," he had often wondered, "the strangeness of these adolescent minds?"

Lantagnac had watched the education of his sons and daughters only from a distance. He knew their basic selves, their qualities of temperament, but little or nothing of the development of their minds. Since their success had always reassured him as to their level of intelligence, he had refrained from pursuing his investigations any further. And now he was discovering, particularly in two of them, he did not know what unfortunate imprecision, what strange disorder in their thinking, what incoherence in their intellectual personality: a kind of inability to follow through with good reasoning, or to concentrate differing impressions and slightly complex ideas around one central point. There seemed to be two souls within them, two spirits which, in turn, each held the upper hand. The strange thing was that this mental dualism showed itself particularly in William and Nellie, the two in whom the well characterized type of the Fletcher heritage stood out as clearly dominant. Wolfred and Virginia, on the other hand, revealed almost exclusively features peculiar to the French: the fine, tanned features of the Lantagnacs and the well-balanced physical conformation, whereas the elder girl and the younger boy, both of whom were fair of hair and complexion, rather slender and a bit lanky, had a striking resemblance to their mother.

"So once again the internal forms of life, the traits of the soul, have moulded the fleshly envelope," the poor father remarked to himself.

Lantagnac remembered that earlier his discovery as to the mental make-up of his children had filled him with consternation. Involuntarily he had recalled a phrase of Barrès: "The blood of races remains identical through the centuries!" And the unfortunate father often surprised himself brooding over the painful reflection:

"So brain disorders and double personalities may be true when races mingle!"

He also recalled a terrible remark of Father Fabien, one day when they were both discussing the problem of mixed marriages:

"Who knows," the priest had said, with a rather blunt frankness, "who knows if our old Canadian nobility did not owe its downfall to the intermingling of strains which it too readily accepted and too often sought? A psychologist would certainly have found it most interesting to observe their descendants. Doesn't it seem to you, my friend, that there is something murky, extravagantly anarchistic, in the past of those old families? How do you explain the frenzy, the wild exhilaration with which the scions of those nobles precipitated themselves into dishonour and ruin?"

On that day Lantagnac, strongly impressed by the priest's energetic tone, and the implacable truth that sprang from his words, had not been able to find an answer. Furthermore, Father Fabien had slipped a little book into his pocket, saying to him:

"You know, I don't believe this Dr. Le Bon more that I should. But one of these days, Lantagnac, when you have a moment to yourself, I ask you to read closely the pages turned down at the corners. For once, I believe the pernicious doctor has spoken well. Besides, all he has done is to sum up the most recent ethnological conclusions."

These pages, which he had read at the time and which had left him so bitterly pensive, he wanted to read them again, now that his own observations made plain to him their painful truth. That evening then, Lantagnac took from his bookcase the tiny volume by Dr. Gustave Le Bon entitled *Lois psychologiques de l'évolution des peuples* and read on pages 59, 60 and 61 the following passages marked with a red pencil:

> Cross-breeding may be an element of progress among superior races who are very close, such as the English and the Germans of America. It always constitutes an element of degeneration when these races, even superior ones, are too different.

> To cross two peoples is to change at one and the same time their physical and mental constitutions . . . In the beginning, the characteristics thus remain very undetermined and weak. A long process of accumulation by heredity is always necessary to stabilize them. The first effect of cross-breeding between different races is to destroy the essential elements of those races, namely that ensemble of common ideas and feelings which make up the strength of peoples, and without which there is neither nation nor native land . . . It is therefore with reason that all peoples who have reached a high degree of civilization have carefully avoided mingling with foreigners.

Lantagnac closed the book again. For a long time, sitting in his armchair by his lamp, he remained musing, weighing bitterly the responsibilities resulting from his marriage, and the infatuations of his youth that had led up to it.

"That," he said to himself, "was the great mistake of my life. And that mistake is irreparable."

These fruitless reflections, arising after so many painful incidents, would, he feared, get the better of the resolutions he had made at Saint-Michel.

"What's the use," he continued to say to himself, "what's the use of risking so much for an undertaking that is bound to fail? There are two of them, perhaps three, who will never be able to become French. I can see it now: there are human entities which it is too late to take apart. Through the upbringing these children have received, the language they have spoken exclusively, the determinism of the heritage that weighs on them, a sort of inescapable discipline has consolidated for ever their ways of thinking and feeling, their ways of conceiving the fundamental problems of life; a rigid law has relentlessly shaped the casts of their minds."

The temptation did not stop there. Lantagnac began to doubt his own conversion. His beautiful memories, and the emotions he had felt at Saint-Michel, gradually faded away, like the perfume of a flower severed from its roots and rapidly finishing its artificial life in the water of a vase. Each weekend, everything had conspired to make him miss his visit to Father Fabien. The atmosphere which surrounded him constantly in his chambers, at the office, in the clubs, on the golf course, in the drawing rooms where he still met his former acquaintances, everything made his new life into an accident rather than a habit. Sometimes, under the growing weight of the indolence that was taking hold of him, he even told himself in desperation:

"No, it's useless, I'll never get over it. I'm carrying in my veins, like a poison impossible to eliminate, the full dose of the drug that has anaesthetized my generation."

[IV]

It was around the end of November, about five o'clock in the afternoon, and office workers were heading home. A cold, gusting wind was sweeping the season's first snow. Thin flakes filled the air, falling endlessly, carried and whirled along pell-mell. The snow went on advancing, very rapidly, like a huge swarm of white bees; then, pushed by the wind, it suddenly changed direction, eddied and turned on itself, like a broad ribbon of light tulle twisted by the squall. It was soft and wet. Children in the street greeted it with joy. Some ran, open-mouthed, to catch the melting manna; others scooped it up from the ground, pressed it, and moulded it in their hands to make balls like pomegranates; and the white projectiles flew from one sidewalk to the other.

Office workers, surprised by the storm, sullen and chilly, with their coat collars turned up and a white fleece on their backs, hastened towards their streetcars. At the corner of Elgin and Sparks Streets, a large gathering had formed before a newspaper placard. Crowded together, the passers-by were reading the day's news item. Young newspaper vendors were waving *The Citizen, The Journal* and *Le Droit*. They were shouting at the top of their voices the big headline that the papers of the capital would make known that evening or tomorrow throughout the whole country: *Grave incident over school question. Senator Landry resigns as Speaker of the Senate.*

Lantagnac, whose chambers were two doors away, also stopped before the placard. The shock moved him to the depths of his being.

"Already!" he said to himself.

He reflected a moment, then added:

"If Landry has brought himself to this supreme decision, that means serious events must be in the offing."

Indeed, a new and dramatic episode of the battle being waged in Ontario over the enactment of the famous Regulation XVII, was about to be played out. Everyone in Canada remembers the principal clauses of this Regulation. The real aim of the law, an end hypocritically concealed behind the preliminary considerations, had been the gradual elimination of French teaching in the bilingual schools of the province of Ontario. French was to be the language of the classroom only in a transitory way: just long enough to allow young French Canadians to learn English. As for the teaching of French itself (grammar, dictation, composition, etc.), the law restricted it to one hour a day, not for each class, but for each school. Even then the use of this paltry privilege was dependent upon the consent of a Protestant inspector, who could, moreover, authorize it only in the bilingual schools set up before the enactment of the Regulation.

That evening, instead of hopping on a streetcar, Lantagnac headed for the interprovincial bridge. He was going to Hull, to see Father Fabien. A quiver of shame mingled with pride tensed his nerves. The senator's heroic action made him ashamed of his lukewarmness and cowardice. "Here's someone," he reflected, "who musn't have met only with approval, either from the members of his family or from his political friends. But there it is! He has been guided only by his conscience and the interests of his cause."

Lantagnac thought about this old man of seventy throwing

in his leaders' faces the honorary title by which they hoped to leash him. The senator was jettisoning honours so as to remain faithful to honour.

"What a stinging blow to the face of the politicians! What an encouragement for those who are fighting!" soliloquized the lawyer. "And how long it is since our political stage has seen such a gesture!"

He had already reached the grey stone Oblate residence. Fortunately Father Fabien was at home. He even said to his visitor:

"I was waiting for you."

The priest was speaking the truth. The day before, at the time when he had made his resignation public, the senator had come to see him:

"We need men," he had said, pressing forcefully. "We need Lantagnac. If you have some influence on him, Father Fabien, now's the time to use it. I have seen him; I've done what I could; he's hesitating."

"I expect him before long," the priest had replied; "it's rather a long time since he's come. If there is some grave decision to be made, he will come."

So when they were seated facing each other, when Father Fabien had gently teased the lawyer for being sparing of his visits, and when Lantagnac had justified himself by referring to the increase in his work, and the bad luck he had invariably encountered whenever he had planned to run over to Hull:

"Well," said the priest, "you've read the big news, and that's what brings you?"

"It is, as you say sometimes, the occasion, not the cause."

"Isn't Landry's gesture a fine one? Better still, superb?" resumed Father Fabien, throwing out his chest as if to catch a breath of an air charged with heroism.

"Superb!" repeated the lawyer, without emphasis, but with a clear simplicity.

Then, questioning in his turn: "But what's happening, then?

The senator is too candid and too noble minded to act a part. If he is resorting to such means, could it be that this is what is now required?''

"Indeed, it is the time for great means," said the priest. And he gravely opened one of his table drawers and handed Lantagnac a document with the words *Strictly Confidential* printed across the corner; then he went on:

"You may read it."

Lantagnac did so. The document revealed the intervention of certain church dignitaries in the Ontario school conflict. In a brief dated August 1910 — this was the document Lantagnac was reading now — these dignitaries declared themselves "alarmed" concerning the future of the Catholic school system in Ontario, "because of the unrest of which the culminating point had been the gathering of French Canadians held in Ottawa in January 1910". Following this strange deformation of facts, the authors proceeded to a decision no less strange: they delegated one of their number to go to see Sir James Whitney, the prime minister of Ontario, in order to inform him "of their entire opposition" to the wishes of the participants of the meeting of French Canadians held in Ottawa in respect of education.

Lantagnac handed the document back to the priest:

"I understand," he said simply.

Lantagnac was one of those who, at the beginning, had believed that the seriousness of the persecution in Ontario was somewhat overestimated. This document revealed to him in a decisive fashion the existence of an hostility which doubled the perils for his compatriots. Father Fabien began to speak again:

"We have long sensed that hostility, my friend, and long feared it. This document, which has come to us from a reliable source, finally gives us the authentic and undeniable proof. Do you understand now that the situation is serious? Against us stand not only the Orange element, but those others who signed that brief.''

The priest heaved his shoulders in a expression of deep sadness.

"Waged in this way," he said, "the battle becomes dangerous and painful. We need strong but prudent leaders. At all costs, we must save the French Catholic schools of Ontario: and at all costs we must save as much as possible the respect for a great authority. Do you see then, my friend, the tragic character that the battle takes on for our compatriots who are worthy sons of the Church?"

"I see," said Lantagnac, "and I understand why the senator has devoted himself to it right to the end."

"There are also the persecuted to be supported," continued the priest. "And I know that the senator has thought of them. The battle has already lasted for six years; it has been harsh for this slumbering people. For them to maintain their courage, they need examples of courage. There is also public opinion to be kept on the alert; great sacrifices will perhaps be necessary before too long, I warn you, Lantagnac, great sacrifices that some of us, those who are leaders or may become so, will have to accept. If Landry has sacrificed himself, it is, I suppose, that he wants to have the right to ask for sacrifice."

Here the voice of Father Fabien, the man of prompt, blunt decisions, took on an incisive, authoritarian tone:

"Lantagnac, you will do me this justice: I take no part in the sorry business of politics; but I readily support the French cause, particularly when it is also a religious cause. So I come straight to the point: you have seen Landry? How does that man inspire you, and may I know what you have decided?"

"I saw the senator," began Lantagnac, in his calm, measured tone; "he's a man as I like them: a man with honest eyes and an honest mind. No affectation, no bombast. Above all, a fine intelligence, perceptive, resourceful, and matching his noble character. In a word, a man who inspires security, the kind of person we have become unaccustomed to seeing."

Then, anticipating Father Fabien's question which he foresaw, he added:

"The senator made me a rather serious overture. A by-election will soon take place in the riding of Russell; he wants me to seek election. It appears that the next act in the school question might well be played out in the federal Parliament. The senator did me the honour of asking for my services."

"And you have accepted?" asked Father Fabien.

"Not yet," answered Lantagnac, in the same calm tone. "Is it faint-heartedness on my part? I am afraid of the consequences of such an action, afraid of the repercussions it may have in my home. You understand me, I think?"

"Lantagnac," replied the priest somewhat solemnly, "we ask you only one thing: that you carry out your duty. That you reconcile your conduct with your recent beliefs, as your gentleman's loyalty, more than any words of mine, I know, urges you to do."

In Father Fabien the man of action never gave up. An impatient, imperious will impelled him towards immediate results. Straight off he set about drawing up a programme of public life for his lawyer friend. For him, Lantagnac's acceptance was not in doubt, any more than his election. The obstacles? The priest waved them away in advance. In a broad synthesis, he summed up for his listener's benefit the racial struggles since the Conquest; he dwelt particularly on the school conflicts since Confederation. He dismissed all the obscurities, all the ambiguities, he went straight after what he called "the fundamental idea of the persecutors"; he laid it bare and concluded vehemently:

"People can blind themselves if they like. But the truth, Lantagnac, the perceptible, visible, tangible truth, the truth that the facts place bluntly before the mind, is that there is in this country a relentless intention to eliminate us as a nationality. What does it matter that the war is conducted by skirmishes, if the skirmishes achieve the objects of a full-scale battle? I tell you: the object is to eliminate us as a people. What is the aim of the countless obstructions to the teaching of

French, in all provinces in which we are in a minority? They are aiming at this or at nothing at all. Where is the niggardliness of the federal government with regard to the French language leading us? Why all these continual infringements of Article 133 of the Constitution, which yet proclaims the legal and political equality of the two languages? I say again, whom do they want to suppress? What do they wish to achieve if not to drive us, from one abdication to the next, to final and total resignation? For after all, if a people continued to infringe upon the territory of a neighbouring country, what would we deduce, in tactical terms, from such repeated raids? It would be said, and rightly so, that it wanted first war, then conquest.

Father Fabien stopped for a moment, in a defiant pose, as if he had to ward off an adversary. Then, in a still more trenchant voice:

"Here, in Ontario, we are being forced to make a final move. It is the most serious of our battles over schooling. Neither in Manitoba nor in the West does the struggle take on such importance. Here the fate of a quarter of a million French Canadians is at stake. Ontario is the first buttress of Quebec; it is so by its geography and its numerical strength. If we, of the Ontario marches, lose this engagement, I tell you, Lantagnac, I don't see how we can win the ultimate battle. Well! do you see, as I talk to you at this moment, what stand the great of heart should take? Do you see it? Promise me at least to reflect on it well."

"I have already begun," said the lawyer, who had followed Father Fabien's speech with great anxiety. He rose to take his leave:

"Rest assured, Father," he felt impelled to add, in a voice that trembled slightly, "rest assured that I shall shrink from no legitimate sacrifice in the carrying out of my duty."

"No legitimate sacrifice"! No doubt he had purposely stressed the adjective "legitimate".

Since the evening of his talk with Virginia, and particularly since that other evening when Maud had said to him, in a fit of weeping, "Our happiness is ended", Lantagnac had lived very few days of real calm. He was not unaware of Maud's autocratic character, which was really inclined to extreme decisions. He knew what advice she would receive in her social world and her English milieu, and in the Fletchers' home itself. From then on he had vowed to be more prudent. At the time, he had planned to have a frank talk with his wife. Then, the fear of provoking irreparable words between her and himself had deterred him; he had postponed it, put if off indefinitely. The result was that each day he had felt himself intimidated, held back by the kind of puritanical reticence in which intimate things are too often shrouded in Anglo-Saxon households. Yet he felt that this situation could not last. To postpone a problem is not to solve it. And on that November evening, as he was hastening towards Wilbrod Street, Jules de Lantagnac turned over in his mind the same obsessive problem:

"I have promised to give Landry my answer tomorrow," he thought to himself. "I shall then have to confide my intentions to Maud, and make her accept my reasons. And what if she rejects them? Supposing she forbids me to stand for election? Supposing she resorts to threats?"

He arrived home at supper time. One of Maud's brothers-in-law, William Duffin, a lawyer at the Ottawa bar, was at the house that evening. He sat down at the table, beside his sister-in-law, and opposite Lantagnac. Duffin, who was fond of talking and talked much, and whom Lantagnac sometimes teased unmercifully, preferred, as he said, to deal with blows that came straight at him, rather than from an oblique angle.

William Duffin was verging on fifty. The son of an Irish emigrant who had come to Canada during the typhus epidemic, Duffin was born at Saint-Michel-de-Bellechasse, where his father, a blacksmith by trade, had long resided. The parish priest had taken a keen interest in the young William, who showed signs of having a lively intellect. He had sent him to college at Sainte-Anne-de-la-Pocatière. The young Irishman became a lawyer, and rapidly acquired a large clientele in Montreal. From then on in close touch with English society, he courted a sister of Maud who had not been converted. His marriage caused him to emigrate to Ottawa. In his new family and his new environment, Duffin, who was of a very pliable nature and very much of an opportunist, soon began to attach little importance to what remained of his French sympathies. His children, who were baptized, went to a public school; he himself had retained no more than a shadow of his faith. The unfortunate Irishman suffered to the highest degree from the *"slave mind"** which had made him, from his earliest contacts, a serf of the Anglo-Saxons, the secular dominators of his race. During the time when he had himself shared in the Anglo-Saxon mystique, Lantagnac had sometimes felt a liking for his brother-in-law; by the same token, now that his illusion had vanished, he felt sorry for this poor victim of assimilation.

The conversation turned first on the commonplace items of the day. They talked of the first snow, and its unexpected coming. Virginia told how the blizzard had caught her downtown, without fur coat or overshoes.

"Alas, my dear, I always expect the snow; it falls summer and winter on my head," sighed Duffin, shaking his mane of white hair in a melancholy but comical way.

"The surprising thing, my dear brother-in-law," observed Lantagnac, as he attacked a cutlet, "is that the snow would stay on a head as excitable as yours."

"Well, at least something does grow on this crater of mine," retorted the Irishman, eying the growing baldness of the master of the house.

"Something?" replied the latter; "yes, a few wispy notions!"

---

*In English in Groulx's original. (Translator's note)

"Did you notice," put in Virginia, "those crowds round the placard, at the corner of Elgin and Sparks? I may be wrong, but I suspect that Senator Landry's resignation is going to cause a lot of talking tonight in Ottawa."

"An unfortunate incident, most unfortunate!" immediately declared Duffin, suddenly becoming annoyed. "If the senator weren't such a worthy man, I would say another rash action!"

Madame de Lantagnac looked towards her husband; they exchanged an embarrassed glance and immediately avoided each other's eyes. Lantagnac looked at his brother-in-law. The latter, keeping his eyes fastened on his plate, was busy eating, at the same time as he continued the discussion. For the moment, only Virginia was holding out against him.

"You have a strange way of assessing courage, Uncle. I believe in a sincerity that proves itself through sacrifices."

"Oh, there's the audience, also, my child," Duffin replied a little harshly; "there's the audience, and the applause that good actors are familiar with, and which intoxicates them. It's a sport like any other. People resign also to get applause."

Lantagnac became a little pale.

"Excuse me, Uncle," said Virginia, speaking again, "it's a sport less popular than golf, and one that usually only men of courage indulge in."

A great golf enthusiast, Duffin was vexed. Did his argumentative mind impel him, that evening, to plunge straight into the discussion for the pleasure of arousing Lantagnac? Or being informed of his brother-in-law's new beliefs, did he mean to test their soundness, to force the neophyte to hoist his colours? Or again, was the artful Irishman playing the first round of a game where he was biding his time in order to win later on? Duffin gave a heavy frown, squared his shoulders abruptly, bent on attack, and started off, half violently; he was still addressing Virginia, but in reality was talking to his brother-in-law:

"Do you want to know, young lady? There are many people in Ottawa, and I'm one of them, who have had enough of this school unrest. For some weeks now, we have been losing count of the heroes. They are being produced in dozens, in fifties; they are being made out of children, boys and girls, eight and ten years old.''

The young girl countered:

''Come on! who's forcing children to be heroic here?''

Duffin pretended not to hear. He went on:

''In a little school on a concession at Renfrew or Prescott, some woman teacher or other, urged on by a few ringleaders, takes the notion of emptying her classrooms on the arrival of the government inspector; the children file out singing the national anthem, or, if necessary, go on school strike by jumping out of the windows. That's all that's required: the next day the papers are full of these exploits and proclaim the birth of forty or fifty new heroes. Isn't it becoming ridiculous?''

''Precisely. Very irritating and very ridiculous,'' cried Virginia, who was getting worked up too. ''Only, dear Uncle, would it be as much so if those young heroes, instead of being little French Canadians of Ontario, were just little English children of the province of Quebec, fighting against a Regulation XVII that barred the English language? Or again, if you prefer, what would Uncle William say, if instead of being the children of the poor inhabitants of Prescott or Renfrew those little strikers were the children of the great lawyer William Duffin, defending their father's language?''

The argument somewhat surprised the Irishman. He did not dare to meet it head on. He contented himself with answering:

''If it were a question of William Duffin's children, William Duffin would begin by teaching them respect for the laws of their province. For the moment we are in Ontario. Ontario is an English land. Why don't the brats learn its language?''

This rejoinder visibly pleased Madame de Lantagnac and Nellie. Neither one was taking part in the discussion. But Lantagnac could not fail to notice that at each of Duffin's sallies his wife and elder daughter found it hard to disguise their satisfaction. As for himself, up to now he had controlled himself. At all costs he wanted to avoid an outburst which would offend his wife needlessly. However, as the argument proceeded, he felt it impossible not to intervene, not to come to the help of Virginia. He would have blamed himself above all for not owning up to his convictions in front of his child, who did it so valiantly. As Duffin was referring again to the violation of the law, and to education in revolution thus being given to the little Franco-Ontarians, Lantagnac could restrain himself no longer. With complete self-possession, which was in total contrast to his brother-in-law's anger, he said:

"The law! the law! Very good, my dear colleague. But suppose we determine first on which side the violators of the law really are?"

Lantagnac's sudden intervention did not appear to surprise Duffin. Accustomed as they both were to crossing swords, Duffin was expecting this entry on the scene. He merely took a defensive stand that was more cautious. In a much milder tone he asked:

"But is it the authorities, the authors and defenders of the law, who are its violators?"

"Why not? The first law, if I am not mistaken, is natural law. And to prevent a people from learning its own language, isn't that violating natural law, against which nothing prevails? Oh, I heard you just now: 'Ontario is an English land; let them learn its language'. But why such evasions? Who, among my people, refuses to learn the English language? Isn't it taught everywhere in our schools, and very effectively, if I am to believe the word of your inspectors? Why then this war on our compatriots, when they ask that in addition to the English language they be allowed to learn French, their mother tongue and the official language of all Canada, by the same right as the other? For that's another thing you forget, my dear colleague," continued Lantagnac, who was gradually becoming animated: "the French language is nowhere foreign in this country. If I go by history and the law, we are here in a bilingual country, bilingual by its ethnic composition, and bilingual by its federative charter. And it might be time for people in your camp to realize once and for all that something happened in 1867, and that French Canadians do not need to ask every ten years for permission to breathe."

"Oh, you are simplifying the case strangely, my dear colleague," replied the other mockingly. "That's one of your habits as a great lawyer. How is it, if the problem is so simple, that you have against you not only the fanatics, the Orangemen, but also all the Irish Catholic element? How is it?"

"How is it? First I note that this unanimity of your people against us, it is you, Duffin, who affirm it. For myself, I prefer to count with gratitude those of your leaders who have nobly hastened to the rescue of the oppressed. If after that the alliance you speak of exists, well, it is none the less an enigma and a mark of shame against a brotherhood."

"Ah, yes!" replied Duffin, who flared up again, "ah, yes, I see what is coming. Go on then. The typhus epidemic! La Grosse-Ile, eh? Our priests, our sisters, devoting themselves like martyrs to helping the poor emigrants, our settlers everywhere taking into their homes the Irish orphans! Go on, my dear fellow. It's so long since we heard that litany!"

"Sorry," interjected Lantagnac, who stopped eating, astounded and sad. "Sorry; I had no intention, my friend, of recalling those memories to you. It's an argument, moreover, that my compatriots are not in the habit of misusing, whatever you may say. 'Brotherhood', Duffin, from my lips, merely meant 'Catholic people'. For after all we have the same faith. And if your leaders had reason to complain about us, and about our schools, why did they not negotiate with our leaders? Why this alliance with the worst enemies of Catholicism in order to crush a minority of French Catholics? Unless I am grossly mistaken, that will one day be the great scandal of history."

Duffin did not answer. Lantagnac went on, visibly moved, in a voice which despite himself had gradually taken on the fullness of oratory:

"You make fun of our heroes? You are wrong. I say, as Virginia did, that those children who go on strike in the face of the inspector, to defend the language of their mothers, are no less admirable than the little Irish boys of old Ireland, Duffin, who brave all punishments in order to learn Gaelic; no less admirable than the little Celts of Wales who allow themselves to be beaten rather than give up speaking Welsh. Why then should what is known as heroism across the ocean be called here comedy?"

Duffin shook his head, disdainfully sceptical.

"Don't take on those airs," said Lantagnac severely. "When, one day, the history of the persecution in Ontario is written, those children that you speak of with scorn, those children of the Renfrew and Prescott concessions, and those of Green Valley, and of Ottawa, and of Windsor, and of Ford City and of New Ontario, will appear as great and as noble as the young Polish children of the Duchy of Posen, and your inspectors and ministers of education as contemptible as the Prussians."

"But really, what are you getting at?" asked his brother-in-law, who still avoided replying directly. "What's supposed to be the outcome of these fruitless struggles and empty words?"

"The outcome?" exclaimed Lantagnac; "the complete victory of my compatriots, unless it be the break-up of Canadian Confederation."

"Oh! no more than that!" said Duffin mockingly.

"Yes. And that's where the oppressors in Ontario are singularly lacking in the most elementary foresight. Let them take note: it is not with impunity that one trifles with racial struggles in a country. Whenever justice is violated it takes its revenge, often a terrible one. One does not make victims with impunity. You, the son of Ireland, should know it better than anyone. A time comes when right-thinking minds and just men, tired of hearing of oppression, more tired still of witnessing it, rise up unanimously, create what is called public opinion, and force the persecutors to disappear into the ground. Or else persecution thinks it triumphs. But it ruins itself as it triumphs. Injustice, once enshrined in custom and become the law governing the mind, means the ruin of authority through contempt: one might as well say the ruin of the deepest foundation of the State. Take my word for it, Duffin; either we shall prevail in Ontario, or the persecutors will destroy Confederation.''

Lantagnac had pronounced these last words forcefully and solemnly. He wondered what would be his brother-in-law's answer. In fact, he believed he had considerably shaken his convictions. Having exhausted his replies, the Irishman could only jeer or resort to fantasy. But Lantagnac's illusion was of short duration. Suddenly he saw Duffin's face go purple; his eyes flashed fire; his voice, a muffled voice to which the stress of a barely disguised hatred gave a tragic note, slowly uttered this menace:

''No, I tell you! it shall not be said that the *Frenchies** of Ontario or Quebec will handle everything in this country as they see fit. They had better look out! If they continue, I warn you, I who am speaking to you: I shall throw myself into the struggle, and I shall not be alone.''

At this unexpected rejoinder, Lantagnac felt his blood rushing to his face. His heart beat harder. A sudden resolution stiffened his will. He picked up the gauntlet:

''As you please, sir; if you go into the struggle, you will find me there. Russell is waiting for a candidate. I have the honour to announce that candidate to you: it will be Jules de Lantagnac.''

---

*In English in Groulx's original. (Translator's note)

Lantagnac had spoken with his eyes fixed on Duffin's. When, after he had finished, he looked round the table, he perceived that Maud had grown pale, and was almost about to faint. Nellie, who was also pale, was feverishly rolling up her serviette. Virginia was inwardly triumphant, but out of consideration for her mother and sister, whose change of countenance had not escaped her, she kept silent. As for Duffin, he seemed to be ashamed of the violent outburst which he had been unable to curb. In a tone completely empty of hostility, and in an almost offhand manner, he replied to his brother-in-law:

"Much good may it do you, my dear fellow; you will certainly be a fine MP"

"I expect success," Lantagnac, already calm and collected, replied.

Then, getting up from the table, he added with perfect graciousness:

"While we're waiting for war, my dear William, let us make good use of peace. You've come for your game of chess? Maud will play with you; you'll lose nothing by the exchange. For myself, I have an important dossier to read through within the next few hours, and some very urgent letters as well to send off. Will you excuse me?"

"Of course, of course," sneered Duffin amiably; "we all know the preoccupations of a parliamentary candidate."

They went into the living room.

It was a spacious room, furnished with an elegance that had been hastily learned. Elaborate lighting set off its slightly heavy opulence. Lantagnac, who had always left to Maud the furnishing of his house, liked it less and less. Now that everything was leading him back towards the orderliness of the French, he looked with growing distaste at this accumulation of odd pieces of furniture and knick-knacks: consoles and period armchairs were somewhat unhappily matched with ottomans and modern armchairs of very doubtful taste.

Curtains and lacquer-ware in colours that were too dark completed the arrangement.

A few minutes later everyone was at his accustomed post. In the middle of the room, the two players, leaning silently over the chessboard, were becoming engrossed in their calculations. Duffin, his hands resting on the edge of the table and his chest bent forward, was feverishly following Maud's moves; he gave little further thought to the earlier argument. Maud, still pale, was concentrating on the game, in order to direct her acute nervous tension into this effort. Nellie, her knitting in her hand, was idly following her mother's play. Lantagnac, settled in a corner of the room near a small cabinet, was writing. It was there that for some time now he had liked to dispose of his urgent business, while remaining partly in contact with the life of his family. Virginia had come to sit near him, and, under her father's lamp, was reading *La Barrière* by René Bazin.

Lantagnac first drafted a very short letter, which he carefully read over. He signed it with a firm hand, and showed it for a moment to Virginia, who smiled and gave her father a look of radiant pride. Next, in his tall, upright handwriting, he addressed the document: *To the Honourable Senator Joseph Landry, the Senate, Ottawa,* and rang for a servant:

"Here," he stressed, "by special messenger, and don't forget."

Then, leaning back in his armchair, an enormous dossier in his hand, he slowly turned over the pages, while his thoughts wandered, sometimes a long way from what he was studying. It was that same evening, at exactly ten o'clock, that the senator was awaiting his reply. His decision now taken, and his letter of acceptance written and sent, Lantagnac felt greatly relieved.

"Father Fabien and the senator will be pleased with me," he said to himself.

However, the consequences of his action could not but

worry him a little. Despite himself, his eyes often turned towards the woman who was playing chess, there opposite him, in a silence strongly revealing of a great internal disquiet. Under the centre lamp he could see the clean lines of her profile; she appeared to him, with her fair hair, in her quiet and still youthful beauty. A hard, obstinate expression was given to her face by the brow, which was set at too perpendicular an angle, and by the lips, which were too tightly drawn and too thin; in contrast, the eye-lashes, too downcast and too mobile, quickly betrayed the slightest sadness. Lantagnac studied Maud, whose state of anxiety was all too visible. He was a kind-hearted man, and he realized at that moment how he would begin to love her, with a stronger love, if she became really unhappy. But that evening, one puzzling thing preoccupied his mind, and that was Duffin's violent, quite extraordinary explosion during dinner. What inflammable substance had excited the Irishman's mind? How was one to explain that impetuous outburst on the part of a man who was normally so well in control of himself, and was possessed, if anything, of a feline flexibility? Lantagnac examined his brother-in-law; he was still bent over the chessboard, saying only the occasional word. Duffin's profile, in which there was something of the great bird of prey, stood out also in clean lines, under his white thatch of hair. Lantagnac was familiar with this type of Anglicized Irishman, for he had often encountered it in his social circle.

"Neophytes are always excessive like that," he reflected. "In that respect, they are no different from us Canadians of the same persuasion."

Lantagnac had seen himself too close to that frame of mind, on certain days, for the ugliness of it to have escaped him. Often, since his conversion, he had pondered over the psychology of the "assimilated".

"What a grievous debasement of the human state!" he remarked to himself.

He had observed that all those so afflicted whether through a desire to win forgiveness for their very recent adhesion to the doctrines of the assimilators, or through a natural hatred for those of their race whose loyalty was a perpetual reproach to them, could be recognized by a common feature, their bitter, fierce zeal for the cause of their new masters. Lantagnac even came to wonder whether the supreme destiny of great imperial races is not to drag behind their chariots these cohorts of self-appointed slaves, those who love their chains. Exactly opposite him, on the wall of the living room, stretched a long engraving towards which he had just cast a glance; the lawyer's reflections were reinforced, at that very moment, by its depressing symbolism. He looked at this Roman bas-relief which displayed the ascension of an imperator to the Capitol. A familiar picture, which this evening took on a new sense, with its long files of mercenary musicians, the conquered of yesterday, who were advancing in measured step, and sounding the hosanna of the conqueror on their long trumpets.

Lantagnac, as we have said, had never gone so far as to despise his race. His noble spirit had been untouched by a proselytism based on hatred. When he looked back to the origin of his conversion to patriotism, he could not conceal from himself that his first aversions had come to him from the cringing speeches and the over-subservient attitudes of certain Irishmen and Anglicized Canadians.

However, if the psychology of the assimilated was the reason for Duffin's violent words, it did not explain the Irishman's threat to throw himself into the struggle. Lantagnac found it hard to imagine his brother-in-law, a speaker with a falsetto voice, which a simple draught could reduce to silence, engaging in the combats of public life and giving of himself unsparingly in public meetings. But then what kind of struggle would he want to undertake, wondered Lantagnac. In fact, he reflected, the school battle was hardly being waged openly, on the enemy side. At that point he recalled that Duffin enjoyed considerable credit in certain English-speaking circles of the capital. In a variety of clubs and drawing rooms, Duffin, a great "joker", had a reputation as an arbiter of wit. As Lantagnac knew, the French Canadians had everything to fear from such gilded society.

"So I shall have to keep my eyes wide open in that direction," he concluded.

For the time being, he had enough anxiety over the state of his wife's soul. How would she accept his candidacy, and after that his position and rôle as a politician? Events would immediately place the lawyer in the forefront of the leaders of French irredentism. Did this not mean his being drawn permanently into a world of ideas and feelings which seemed to be more and more repugnant to Maud? By what means could he manage to reassure her, to save the little that remained to them both of the peace of their home? Lantagnac felt indeed that he had already delayed too long. He could no longer put off talking to his wife.

"I owe it to myself," he thought, "to come to an understanding with Maud. I shall have to do it tomorrow evening at the latest. The day after tomorrow I leave for my riding, and shan't return until the election is over."

He did not have to take the initiative. The next day the newspapers of the capital published on their front pages, in bold headlines, the candidacy of Jules de Lantagnac in the riding of Russell. The great lawyer's entry into politics naturally made a tremendous stir. This independent candidacy was inevitably linked to the resignation of Senator Landry; it was taken as a sign of the intention of the Ontario minority to strengthen its leadership and perhaps to strike a decisive blow. Comment was rife.

Nowhere was stupefaction more intense than in the Fletcher family. Maud's father, an accountant with the Department of Finance, an old career civil servant, who had himself succeeded his father in the job, could not believe his eyes that

afternoon when he opened *The Journal*. Lantagnac, his
son-in-law, an independent candidate, and in the French riding
of Russell! The worthy old man almost fainted on the old chair
cushion which had been his father's before his. Lantagnac was
someone he basically esteemed. For old Davis Fletcher, his
son-in-law was almost a great man. Endowed with talent and
wealth, and so unreservedly won over to the ''superior race'',
Maud's husband might become a senator, perhaps a minis-
ter. . .! The choice would be his. And then what good
sinecures for the budding little civil servants of the Fletcher
line! And what a glorious day for papa Davis, if one of his
grandsons were to occupy his venerable accountant's seat, and
perpetuate the family dynasty! It was an exalted, soothing
dream, with which the old man, in the dark, damp days of
spring and autumn, liked to warm his aging heart and his
rheumatic gout. Of course, the Fletcher family had, for some
time, found the behaviour of its son-in-law a little strange.
William's going to the University of Ottawa had caused
surprise, almost indignation. Fortunately, Lantagnac's com-
mon sense had quickly rallied, and the boy had returned to
Loyola College. But that the great lawyer should have come to
concern himself with that wretched school question, and have
given the *Frenchies** of Ontario the support of his oratory and
prestige, wasn't that the last thing one might have expected?

"Oh, shocking, oh, very bad!"* old Davis Fletcher kept on
repeating dolefully, that afternoon.

He went round the office, tearful and crestfallen, showing
the others the newspaper headlines; and as he hastened from
one to the other, in his pitter-pattering gait, his wizened,
parchment-like face appeared ever greyer and more colourless.

On the old man's sensibility, aggravating his sorrow and
anger, the two formidable passions of the Anglo-Saxon,
material interest and nationalistic pride, were acting in unison.

---

*In English in Groulx's original. (Translator's note)

When he returned home, at five o'clock, the scene began again. Maud was there, having come for advice. The conversation quickly turned to Lantagnac, who was blamed violently and condemned without abatement. At first, against her own feeling, Maud ventured a timid defence of her husband, then said no more when Jules's conduct was presented to her as a challenge to the Fletcher clan and its loyalty, and as an act of contempt against his wife's most intimate and sensitive feelings. Old Fletcher flung aside all restraint; he became abusive; all the old clichés about Francophone fanaticism came out.

Old Davis went further: Maud must use all her influence to get Jules's candidacy in Russell withdrawn. If necessary, she must resort to the ultimate threats. What sort of married life was this, where husband and wife were divided on essential issues?

"If your heart's in the right place," old Davis ventured to say, "you will stop this scandal that is ruining us all, and you know how to."

Would Maud obey this imperious injunction? Would she dare to utter the decisive word so soon? For some days now, the poor woman had been feeling herself a prey to the most tumultuous feelings. At first, this unprecedented shock, which mercilessly shattered her security and her happy unconcern, had left her not knowing where to turn. Whence came this wind of ill omen, which after twenty-three years withered the unruffled charm of her life, as the icy blast of autumn robs the green leaf of its colour in a single night? But after the outbursts of anger and the admonishments of her father, and under the influence of a grief too long harboured, she felt now that a relentless passion was stiffening her will and exacerbating her sensitivity. And she made no mistake about this passion: it was indeed, through a natural impulse for reprisal, the spirit of her national background which made her rise to the defence of her children.

That same evening, when Virginia and Nellie had gone to their rooms, Lantagnac was preparing to start his explanation, but Maud had forestalled him. He saw her, with *The Journal* in her hand, pull up her armchair quite close to his. She was pale, and her lips were drawn together.

"Jules," she began in a slightly trembling voice, "is this news really true and final?"

She opened *The Journal* out before him.

"Yes," he said, endeavouring to keep calm. "I gave my reply last night; I'm leaving tomorrow for my riding."

"My dear," replied Maud, still more sadly, "couldn't I have expected to be consulted on such a serious matter?"

"It didn't rest with me, my dear Maud," consoled Jules, genuinely distressed by his wife's sorrow. "Yesterday, as you know, William was here; he monopolized our evening. Then you remember our discussion at table. You know me, Maud; I believe I have a gentleman's sense of honour, which cannot be provoked with impunity. I confess the truth honestly to you: last night, I was still hesitant, even seriously hesitant about standing for election. In the face of Duffin's declaration of war on my compatriots, I should have considered that I was being disloyal to the honour of my blood if I had not picked up the gauntlet with a flourish."

These last words caused a slight redness to come into his wife's cheeks. Her husband had just brought her back to the painful reality, to this change in his state of mind which separated them irrevocably. Maud's voice grew firmer; an expression of defiance appeared in her eyes and on her lips. Lantagnac realized that the assault of tenderness was about to give way to other feelings, the dangerous passion of this private drama which pitted them a little more each day one against the other. Hence it was with a curt voice that Maud retorted:

"I knew a time, Jules, when concern for your compatriots did not find you so touchy."

"Do me justice, Maud," Lantagnac flung back, with a

barely disguised sharpness; "I pitied my people; I never despised them."

"No," said Maud, still annoyed; "but you spoke readily at that time of a superior race that was not yours."

"Oh, that I grant you; but there is something changed in my spirit."

"I knew it; you are no longer the same since your famous trip to Saint-Michel. And your wife, in your eyes, now has the fault of belonging to the inferior race."

Lantagnac made a slight gesture of impatience.

"Maud, my dear," he continued in an entreating manner, "shall we talk in a different tone? What's the use of our trying to wound each other in our most sensitive spots, when in reality, as you well know, I haven't changed towards you?"

"Be honest, Jules," she answered coldly, almost provokingly; "the blood that flows in the veins of Maud Fletcher could not become less pure, could not take second rank in your esteem, without your wife falling also."

"Why do you talk of a superior and an inferior race? I still believe in the superiority of yours; furthermore, I also believe in the superiority of mine; but I consider them different, that's all. If you ask me to which of the two my preference goes, respect my feelings, Maud, as I respect yours."

Madame de Lantagnac shrugged her shoulders:

"As you respect mine, you say? How can I believe in such respect, when you have decided that my children should be French?"

Maud folded her arms, awaiting the reply, knowing that she had just uttered the decisive statement, the one that summed up the whole situation between them. And as Lantagnac continued to look at her, his face reflecting despite himself an unspeakable anguish, she continued:

"For twenty years you left to me, to me alone, the education of those children. Tell me, did I fail in my duty, since all at once you decide to take them from me?"

"Take them from you!" he cried. "Reserving for myself

the part in them that belongs to me, is that taking them from you? Once again, my dear Maud, let's not use this sort of language, which is too new for us. You know well enough that I haven't committed the grave crime you reproach me with. You are still the beloved mother of my children. But after all, aren't those children of French descent on their father's side? Maud, I will not hide it from you: I want none of my sons, none of my daughters, to be able to reproach me later for the greatest crime that a father can commit against his children, after having deprived them of their faith: to cut them off from their forbears.''

Madame de Lantagnac appeared somewhat confounded. She detected in these words the expression of a will that she knew was as unrelenting as it was inflexible. The shock to her pride was too strong, and pushed her to extremes. She assumed the rôle of those who, having exhausted the possibility of argument, can only fall back on aggravating their own error. In a still more curt and imperious voice, she went on:

''I understand you, Monsieur de Lantagnac, I understand you. You take away from me the soul, the heart and the mind of my children; the rest, if any, you leave to me. And that you do deliberately, breaking my heart in the process, something which for you is no doubt unimportant. But you do it also at the expense of the harmony between our children, which means destroying the peace of our home.''

Lantagnac made a supreme effort to control himself. He felt that, at that moment, merely a word or a gesture could wreck all the happiness of his existence, the very foundations of his home life. In a very restrained and sorrowful tone he said, resting his forehead on his hand:

''Maud, one day you will blame yourself for your harsh words, and the injustice that you are doing to me, I hope involuntarily. On whom among my children have I used compulsion? Whom have I forced to learn French? William decided to return to Loyola College; he is there. Wolfred is at the French university in Montreal; God is my witness that he went there on his own accord. Nellie wants to continue her English education; is she my child any less, and have I loved her the less for it? Finally Virginia is complying, freely also, with my desires; she will be the most French of the family. Well, knowing how she feels, I say this in her favour: she does not love her mother, her sister and her brothers more than she loves others, perhaps, but no one loves the members of her family more than she does. No, Maud, one does not demean oneself by reverting to oneself, by reconstructing within oneself the ancient, natural soul that one inherited. What I have done, I had hoped to do without causing you the slightest grief.''

On hearing this word, Madame de Lantagnac stood up. She believed she held the weapon of victory:

"If you are sincere, Jules, you will not want to cause me further grief. Tell me that you are giving up the candidacy.''

She stood there, with the newspaper in her hand, her face quivering with emotion, ready to go to any lengths if her husband's lips framed a refusal. Lantagnac looked at her for a moment, poised in that frightening attitude. He passed his hand across his brow, trying to find the words or the phrase which would save everything. In a strangled voice he replied:

"Maud, would you love me still if I dishonoured myself?''

This answer did not disarm the unhappy woman.

"So,'' she stressed, "you refuse?''

"Maud,'' resumed Lantagnac, distraught, "ask me for any other proof of affection, but not that one. Have you considered it, my dear? Withdraw from the struggle, at the time when my own kind have so much to endure, when humble folk are accepting such heroic sacrifices for their cause? No, I can't; understand me, I can't retreat like that without neglecting all my duties as a man of honour. You know well enough that in order to justify myself I should place before the public only the motives which are the true ones. And that would be dishonour, for you as for me. No, Maud, I beg you, not that.''

She was still standing, in the same provocative manner. In a voice that grew muffled, with an undertone of concentrated anger, she added:

''And have you weighed carefully what may happen to your home? And do you assume the responsibility?''

Lantagnac stood up in his turn. He took his wife's hands in his:

''Maud, Maud, I entreat you once more, don't utter words that are irreparable.''

She broke away abruptly. Haughtily, in quick steps and without looking back, she went up the main staircase to her room.

[V]

Lantagnac was elected to Parliament for Russell, without the need for a ballot. All candidates stood aside before this formidable opponent. When he returned home, a week later, he was agreeably surprised by Maud's attitude. He was expecting sulkiness, a scene, even something worse. Maud displayed an exemplary correctness. She refrained from congratulating the new member. She even seemed to find rather distasteful the effusive joy of Virginia, who threw her arms round her father's neck and hugged him at length. But she did at least behave with propriety, and Lantagnac was pleased. Maud had sensed around her that a speedy break would be a tactless action. Old Davis Fletcher had quickly elicited from himself another attitude, a way for the venerable bureaucrat of regaining the serenity which was so vital to him. Faced with the inevitable, the civil servant's instinct for the practical had sought the best way of adjusting to it. The old man had said to himself:

"Lantagnac has talent; he even has a great deal. As an independent, he will give anxiety to the government, which will do all it can to win him over. In short, he's taking a step back to gain more ground, and to gain it more quickly. Don't independence and talent open up the road to honours? That often happens."

Thus Davis Fletcher had spoken to his daughter, Maud. He had added:

"Furthermore, Lantagnac sits in the federal Parliament. The French matter, as you know, is being debated in Toronto, not here. In the end, what will your husband do for his people? He will preside over small meetings, perhaps even large ones: so many harmless things. Besides, all his friends, all those he associates with, still come from among our people. That environment will always prevent him from doing foolish things. No, dear daughter, we must be careful not to precipitate anything. Time helps many things. And supposing Lantagnac became powerful, entered the cabinet. . . who knows? My succession would be sure to go to one of our kin, your son William, perhaps."

Maud had promised to have patience and to be prudent. Basically, her father's words had only half reassured her. Her feminine clear-sightedness led her to fear the worst from Jules's too absolute sincerity. Would not a mind entirely ruled by logic and loyalty go right to the end of its convictions? And who would check the will of a man on the road where an unmistakable duty had launched him?

At first the member for Russell appeared to confirm old Fletcher's expectations, at least partially. Lantagnac had realized that authority, in parliamentary circles as elsewhere, is the reward only of competence. He had set to work again in earnest. He studied everything in order to be able to speak on all topics. He familiarized himself with financial questions, where he had quickly perceived the limitations of the French MP's. Convinced, in addition, that intellectual power was a matter less of the extent of one's knowledge than of the creative vigour of one's mind, he devoted himself to wide but intensive reading. As a layman eagerly pursuing the highest enlightenment, he was deterred by nothing, whether philosophy or even theology.

"A trifle more," Father Fabien said to him one day, as he

gave him a volume of Father Pègues's commentaries on Aquinas, "a trifle more, and you'll be taking my whole library home with you."

Intelligent, the product of a fine, healthy lineage, Lantagnac benefited, as Renan said of himself, from all the mental vitality saved up by six generations of farm labourers. These first months of his parliamentary life were beyond question the most active period of his life as an MP. He was one of the most faithful in his attendance at the sittings of the House, and from time to time, when he felt himself master of a subject, he would speak. In this atmosphere, which was so different from that of the courts, he practised aiming his voice and finding the right pitch. From the earliest days, the ministers could not refrain from listening. In the front rows on the right, heads looked up with greater attention when his words rang out, words that were always clear, full of substance, and uttered with an impeccable distinction. Soon the opinion was established, in political circles, that nothing would prevent the member for Russell from reaching the heights if such was his wish.

Unfortunately for the Fletchers, the assurance that Jules de Lantagnac was willing to concede to their hopes went no further. At the same time, they saw him pursue his intellectual training, and with no less ardour the achievement of his moral being. A feverish ambition was driving this man of real integrity to fill what he called "the frightful void of his earlier life".

"In short," he sometimes reproached himself, "I am accountable to my own people for twenty years of arrears."

He believed in a close solidarity within nations and families, and in the repercussion of both mistakes and good deeds through the generations. When he recalled the capitulation of the Canadian nobility, after the Conquest of 1760, he had the terrible thought of a fatal expiation lying heavily on his own family. Moreover, he feared for his children the peril of wealth, and the peril of an Anglicization that had already begun. What distressing news he had learned in these last few weeks! Wolfred and Nellie were manifestly both heading for the mixed marriage which their father dreaded. This very painful discovery, on which a recent speech of Father Fabien had elaborated, had upset Lantagnac deeply.

"Wouldn't it seem to be a law of nature," the priest had said, "in all nationalities struggling for their being, that the upper classes betray themselves in the very process by which they are formed? Brought into more direct and immediate contact with the conqueror or oppressor, they progressively weaken and succumb: their self-interest leads them to cultivate regular social relations with the aliens; then, under the influence of the richest among them, they gradually yield to the temptations of vanity. That's the second stage: they adopt the fashions, the titles, the decorations that are handed to them as enticement. Next, through pride, or an absence of national faith, they accept marriages, the mingling of blood: this means their downfall and their ruin. No one," the priest had added, in a tone that was sometimes a little sententious, "no one can carry in his soul the ideal of two national entities when the two are in opposition. You recall what happened formerly to our nobility. Isn't the same calamity taking place under our eyes, among the upper bourgeoisie of French Canada? Just look at the ambitious newcomers in politics or finance, who lie in wait for titles and medals, and ready to seize any kind of 'noble' label: or again, those ostentatiously wealthy women, whom the coveted title of 'lady' sends swooning. Look at those silly women in their clubs or at the race-tracks, who consider it more *chic* to speak English. Then tell me, Lantagnac, isn't it among those people that mixed marriages are already rampant, and that betrayals are being perpetrated with appalling speed?"

These imperious tirades of Father Fabien aroused Lantagnac's determination. He who had mixed with this bourgeoisie, he could not but concede the appropriateness of the priest's condemnations, severe though they were. A very clear conclusion asserted itself to him. If he wanted to protect his children effectively, even to save them, if possible, there was not a minute to lose; no sacrifice must be refused. He must, however distasteful this might be, reach to the quick of his own being.

"What's the use," he remarked to himself, "of making my home French, if I do nothing to remove the risk of certain contacts? Who knows if it isn't even somewhat late in the case of Nellie and Wolfred?"

Without waiting any further, the convert set about completing the protection of his home. It was around that time that he took the most energetic resolutions, those that required the greatest will-power. It was also on those occasions, when the rumour of such reactions reached her or when she thought she could sense them, that Maud felt all her fears returning. She followed with a sort of terror the ill-defined course of her husband's thoughts. Often, at the beginning of that winter of 1915, at the sight of a radical change in certain of his habits, or when he refused, as he often did, now, to accompany her among their former social circle, or again, faced with his obsession for shutting himself up in his room on the pretext of ever urgent tasks, Maud would run tearfully to Nellie. In the midst of tears and astonishment, mother and daughter would exchange confidences, determine plans of action that came to nothing, talk anxiously about a future which they contemplated with disquiet.

"My goodness!" Maud would say, "where is this leading us? How long, at this rate, can we continue living together?"

The poor woman would not, alas, have found her apprehensions too great if she had been able to read her husband's private diary at that time. Let us take a look at it. Lantagnac, who was devoid of romantic egotism, wrote in it only his most lasting impressions, at very infrequent dates. But those pages, infrequent though they were, will tell us with what thoroughgoing ardour this man who was French in spirit set about freeing himself from his former ties:

"*15 December 1915:* Can the past be redeemed? A painful remorse grips my heart. I reflect that for twenty-five years, I, a rich lawyer, have given my own kind the evil example of one who denies his origins. In these hours when dark, depressing thoughts whirl around my brow like a cloud of black moths, I sometimes think I see the lineage of the Canadian Lantagnacs, and the whole line of female forbears, filing before me, with their faces veiled and sad. They, I know, poverty not-withstanding, have defended the great heritage of the ancestral soul, and loyalty to one's culture. And I, what have I done? what have I done? Can the past be redeemed?

The other day I pondered for a long time a definition of *race* which I had come across in one of my favourite works. 'Race' is 'a tried and lasting equilibrium of moral qualities and physical habits, which the introduction of a heterogeneous element on a massive scale is liable to break'. Why did that brief formula occupy and stimulate my mind for so long? Because it emphasized for me, in an acute way, the responsibility of those classes which more than the others destroy the 'lasting equilibrium' by the introduction of the 'heterogeneous element'. Since that day, I would dearly like to cry aloud to our forgetful bourgeois who perhaps say: 'What do one or two individuals fewer matter to the collectivity?', I would dearly like to keep riveted before their eyes, like a watchword or a spur to remorse, those thoughts of Edmond de Nevers which are all too true:

Each one of the descendants of the 65,000 conquered in 1760 must count for one . . . Each defection in our midst, each manifestation of a spirit which is no longer the old French spirit, proud, uncompromising, glorious, encour-ages the chimerical notion, so ardently cherished by the pan-Saxonists, of our future assimilation.

And I, have I done all I should to stop the weakening in my own family, to repair my great mistake? I will, in any case, have come to a practical resolution. I don't want a single one of my compatriots, in the future, to be able to quote a single instance of questionable conduct on my part as his authority. I have thought also of my sons, hoping that perhaps one day their feelings, guided by my example, would follow the same course as mine. And here is what I wish to record in my diary, so as to commit myself to it irrevocably: Finished, once and for all, my regular visits to the Country Club! Next spring, no more games of golf in Chelsea and in Aylmer! This decision may seem childish; it cuts me off from all my old friendships, all my old habits, and the pleasures I am the most fond of. It's my break with a world. But I've decided on it; I shall hold to it.

Just today my resolution was put to a sharp test. Maud's father, as it often happened in the past, had asked me to take him to Chelsea. I had to utter my first refusal. The scene took place in his house, in his little den, after dinner. To tell the truth, it was painful. But, after all, clean-cut positions are always preferable.

'No, you haven't reached that point, surely?' he said to me, as he stopped smoking, clearly dismayed.

'Yes,' I replied; 'I have sworn it to myself, as to a man of honour. You will understand me.'

The poor old man couldn't understand anything at all. He stared at me for a few moments, both bewildered and sad. He answered:

'Lantagnac, is it you talking like this? A man like you? With your part to play? Can you, without damaging the very interests you are defending, can you break completely with our environment, and cast yourself into isolation? Can you do it?'

'Break completely? no,' I rectified; 'but I maintain that that social world must no longer be my usual one; it will no longer be so.'

He kept silent, with his head lowered; caught once more in an enigma that frightened him. I went on:

'You, dear Dad, who place your national faith above all else, you will not blame me. Well do I know what these associations with alien environments are worth; they may be harmless, even advantageous for someone who needs good vantage points. They aren't so for me, who have nothing more to learn from them, and whose inner self has, alas, been grievously undermined by them.'

'But has your conversion,' said the old man ironically, 'made you so timid, so worried . . .?'

'Yes,' I retorted, very concerned for my dignity.

'But what's threatening it, then? I don't see it,' emphasized Mr. Fletcher, visibly irritated by this discussion. 'We Anglo-Saxons despise the weak; but we admire the strong.'

'Everyone respects the strong, Papa Davis,' I again corrected him, a little sharply. 'But to the strong, you give only external respect. And sometimes one's dignity is not content with that.'

'What do you mean?'

I had to contrive to reconcile frankness and deference as best I could. Determined however to speak openly, I told him what I really thought:

'What is wrong with your compatriots, whom I admire, dear Papa, as you know, for many of their qualities, is that they have commercialized the human kind. They assess a man, particularly an alien, only at his market value, his value as an instrument. That's what it is for the Anglo-Saxons: the human stock has its quotation on the Stock Exchange like the other industrial and financial shares. And the Stock Exchange quotation is the measure of their esteem. Do you understand me now? Jules de Lantagnac is no longer an instrument to be used. No doubt he will be respected. But he will no longer be the friend, the *nice fellow** he once was. They will hide their

---

*In English in Groulx's original. (Translator's note)

scorn, but it will be there. And you can't, I imagine, frown on Maud's husband's refusal to adjust to that.' Papa Davis sustained this flood of speech without flinching. After a long silence he shook the ash from his cigar, which continued to burn between his fingers; then, with a note of objection in his voice, he exclaimed:

'What a time to be speaking like that, my friend! At the time when we, we, don't you realize? are talking to you of mutual understanding!'

'I know,' I replied, ill concealing my impatience; 'but shall we talk about something else?'

'What, then?' asked the old man, deeply offended. 'Is peace so horrifying to you?'

Once more I hesitated. Then, again, I decided to be frank:

'It is not peace that I'm afraid of.'

'What are you afraid of, then?'

'I am afraid of the mutual deceptions in which naiveté is only on one side, which isn't yours.'

'Meaning . . .?'

'Meaning that so long as there is a despoiler and one who is despoiled one can speak of a truce or an armistice; but neither of mutual understanding nor of friendship; or if the victim of spoliation agrees to use those words, he does so only in the name of his abjection.'

Clearly the old man understood less than ever. His racial pride and his prejudices could not entertain the possibility or the right of French survival in Canada. In all honesty he could not understand that the deprived minority should still have cause to complain, from the moment that the satiated majority offered it the olive branch. His bewilderment increased still further when I added:

'You want to establish friendship between the two national groups? Suppose you start by creating justice? Between your compatriots and mine, Mr. Fletcher, I am afraid there persists a fundamental misunderstanding. Your people, in this country, dream of agreement in uniformity; ours want to maintain it in diversity. There, if you can believe it, is the root cause of all our disagreements, all our misunderstandings, and all our quarrels. True mutual understanding is possible, but on one condition.'

'Which one?'

'That the Anglo-Saxons finally accept the fact of federation, with all its consequences in the political, national, social, and religious realms. Frankly, are they willing, without any further cunning and ambiguity, to give up once and for all their pretension to level everything under the knife of ethnic pride? Are they willing to abandon their claim to a unified country through a unified national entity? That's the whole point.'

Poor old Davis was, for the moment, stunned. He looked at me with eyes that now expressed grief and distress. He threw his extinguished cigar into the ashtray, and began to walk up and down, muttering in real sorrow:

'So that's where he's got to! That's where he's got to!' ''

[VI]

These breaks with old friendships caused Jules de Lantagnac some suffering, as all breaks do; they also brought him some joy. Each time a link with his former environment was broken, his mind felt that a chain was severed. Each day, as he confessed to Father Fabien, he felt more sharply within him the retreat of a stranger, of an intruder whom he was anxious to dislodge completely.

These joys and hopes lessened the irritations of all kinds which beset him daily in his family environment. In their home, the somber reality continued to worsen. Each stage in his emancipation added to the general uneasiness or irritability. Since he had left the Country Club, the Fletchers had practically ceased to see him. With Maud the peace was prolonged. But, as Lantagnac knew only too well, there are feelings that cannot be revived. Morally and physically, nothing is less curable than ills of the heart. Between Maud and her husband, since that evening when their minds had clashed so violently, the last surviving vestiges of their intimacy were dying. The more he became French in spirit, the more the convert could perceive the growing coldness with which his life's companion was surrounding herself.

As for the children, the mere thought of them made him more and more perplexed. Virginia was still the only one who was truly his. Prudent and discreet, she continued unobtrusively to be her father's support. In the evening, during his regular walk on the verandah, she would go and join him, she would tell him what she was reading, and the sense of joy and harmony in her soul, now that it had at last become French again. They spoke together of the pilgrimage they would very soon make to the family's birthplace, to the Lamontagnes at Saint-Michel. And Virginia was exultant at the thought of the stirring memories which the landscape would awaken in her mind. When the member for Russell was due to speak in the House, the dear child never failed to go and take a seat in the gallery, just opposite the speaker, in order to give him praise and encouragement. What was Virginia's future? Lantagnac wondered, with anxious affection. The progress of faith and religious feeling in his child's soul had been still more marked than the development of a French consciousness. Her great happiness, in her free time, was to run over to the Rideau Street Convent, where she attended the French language and literature classes. Sometimes Mademoiselle de Lantagnac would climb on the platform, to deputize for the teacher, something that delighted her. One day when he had entered his daughter's room, Lantagnac had been struck by the large number of religious pictures on the walls. Just opposite Virginia's little writing desk, he had seen in the place of honour, below the crucifix, three medallions, slightly interlocked. In the frame of fine gold he had recognized the face of Marguerite Bourgeoys, that of Jeanne Mance, and in the centre the angelic profile of Jeanne Le Ber, as beautiful as that of little Thérèse of Lisieux. A few faded white roses, obviously placed there in homage to the three heroines of New France, were slowly wilting under the picture.

"What joy or what sorrow might Virginia have in store for me?" Lantagnac had asked himself at the time.

His fatherly anxieties would grow markedly more acute at this period, with the return of the Christmas holidays. What would this coming reunion of his children, who were themselves involved in the silent family drama, turn out to be? How often had Lantagnac recalled those bitter words of Maud, on the evening of their first altercation: "What you are doing," she had said, "you are doing deliberately, breaking my heart, which for you would no doubt be unimportant; but you are doing it also at the expense of the harmony between our children." The poor father often repeated those pitiless words to himself. Often too he wondered, with some distress, to what extent the family drama encompassed and troubled his sons and daughters. Was the gulf between them as deep as their mother said?

Christmas arrived. The boys came back from Loyola and Laval* to Wilbrod Street. Wolfred, enigmatic as always, said little about his stay in Montreal. It seemed that he had imposed upon himself the determination not to reveal any of his impressions. Nor could anyone have detected, as regards the problem in his family, the hidden thoughts of this tall young man with dark, energetic features, who substituted questions for the responses expected of him, and whose eyes, despite their very set, straight gaze, retained an impenetrable veil. As for William, he was still the same obstinate, testy individual. As the younger boy grew older, Saxon characteristics became sharper in the face and the whole body of this lanky adolescent. The line of the brow became more taut, the pout of the lips more arrogant; he would generally amble along, his neck pulled back, his fists half closed, with the gait of a rugby player. Moreover, during the holidays, he made a show of being as often at his godfather William Duffin's house as he was at home. Lantagnac did not much appreciate William's too lengthy and too frequent stays in such a milieu. The most recent events proved that Duffin's war cry had not been an

---

*That is, Laval at Montreal. The Université de Montréal did not exist as a separate entity until 1920. (Editor's note)

empty threat. While the unrest over the schools was intensifying in the capital, one could feel everywhere the same scheming, contriving hand.

The holidays were nearing their end. The poor father, still worried, was beginning nevertheless to hope that they would finish without incident. It was the day after the Epiphany, in the afternoon. William and Wolfred would leave the next day. Madame de Lantagnac was away and would not be back until late evening. Lantagnac had just come home, a little earlier than usual. He was settled in his study, and was begining to read the papers. Suddenly, noisy echoes from a room above came to his ears. He listened; yes, it was the voices of his children. Thinking they were alone in the house, they were arguing heatedly. Lantagnac decided to go and join them. He had scarcely climbed the first step when he stopped short. He had just heard Virginia say:

"Dad is right when he maintains that children should belong to the same ethnic group and speak the same language as their father. Isn't he the head of the family?"

A harsh voice that Lantagnac recognized immediately, William's, interposed:

"Sorry, miss, a father has no business imposing his will in such matters. My godfather put it very well: we have the right to choose, particularly when the option offered implies a kind of loss: the acceptance of an inferior status."

"An inferior status!" answered Virginia; "oh! I like that! Didn't you hear Uncle William congratulate Dad, in this very place, on the advantages of his French culture? He maintained that it makes him the foremost lawyer in Ottawa. You've read the English authors, you said just now; they've filled you with wonder. And I, I ask you: have you read the French authors? Before judging between two cultures, mustn't one first compare?"

"Rubbish! Now one'll have to read a whole library before he has the right to speak," replied William cantankerously.

"Our friend Wolfred here has been indulging in that kind of reading for some time. Come on, is he changed, converted? Let him speak."

Breathing fast, Lantagnac leaned against the banister, waiting for his elder son's reply. Was the mysterious, enigmatic Wolfred at last going to reveal his thoughts?

The reply did not come. William went on:

"But we're crazy to argue so much. What's the good of our opposing power and progress? Is the French survival in Canada anything but a colossal fantasy? Just remember this axiom, that Uncle William told me only yesterday: 'Power and the future belong to the assimilating races. It's an historical argument that is no fallacy. And nothing is equal at present to the assimilating power of the Anglo-Saxon race.' "

"Oh, no, just a minute! I beg your godfather's pardon: if the argument had some value, the example is worthless."

This time it was indeed Wolfred who was speaking. Lantagnac held his breath. The elder son continued:

"You know, I'm not one to let my head be stuffed with sham axioms. Where does your godfather see the success of the Anglo-Saxon race as a great assimilator of peoples? Where? I can pick out some sizeable shortcomings to its triumphs. I note for example that England has truly assimilated neither Ireland, nor even Scotland, nor India, South Africa, Malta, Egypt, or French Quebec. Once again, dear brother, where did you and your uncle make your dazzling discovery?"

"And the Americans, what do you say about them, young man?" interjected William, sure that his objection was a victorious one.

"What do I say, dear boy?" retorted Wolfred, in the same assertive tone. "No more assimilators than the others. There, as everywhere else, a single power has only truly absorbed and blended into itself small ethnic groups, amorphous and disconnected from a political or national point of view, scattered remnants of peoples, in fact. Really, my dear

William, you're a rather dim schoolboy," continued Wolfred mockingly. "For your enlightenment, and to complete your master's lessons, read not a library, but just the book by Edmond de Nevers, *L'Ame américaine*, which is praised by Brunetière, or else *Outre-mer*, by Paul Bourget. And tell me what you think of them."

Here there was a long pause. William, daunted by the dogmatic tone of his elder brother, no doubt found nothing to reply. Nellie broke the silence. In the curt tone of an English governess, she said:

"In any case, my friends, these discussions between us are depressing. For myself, I would willingly give Virginia's Racine and Bossuet for the former peace of the family. In those days, in this house, there was a woman who cried less often."

"Oh, why do you say those things?" entreated Virginia.

"I say them because they have to be said," stressed Nellie.

"And why is it so necessary to say them?"

"To give you good warning. Don't you know that Mother nearly left us out of grief, at the time of the election in Russell? The slightest incident, I know and I'm telling you, could bring about a disaster."

"Exactly," added William. "So what's this new religion that's being preached at us, that aims at separating brother and sister, husband and wife? I think that someone here has taken a long time to notice the superiority of the French. And I have little use for Racine and Bossuet in settling this argument."

Lantagnac, whose heart was beating too fast, came down one step. At that moment, for the second time, the authoritative voice of Wolfred made itself heard:

"Come on, William, you take pleasure in being difficult. Smarten up! Why did you need to start this argument? These are the sort of questions one doesn't bring up here, where Father or Mother could hear us . . ."

Lantagnac returned to his study. He was crushed by

William's words. He clearly recognized in his second son the too faithful disciple of Duffin. And Nellie's allusions to Maud's sorrow and threats? Could he continue to deceive himself? The children were well aware of all the components of the family drama; the danger of separation was indeed only postponed.

Alas! it is a sad privilege of sorrow, that one source of suffering will inflame another. Now that the words he had just heard had revealed to Lantagnac the deep dissension in his home, an incident, on New Year's day, which at the time had only slightly affected him, suddenly appeared as a cruel wound. The facts linked up perfectly, to produce their painful meaning. For that morning, Lantagnac had conceived a dream which was perhaps more of a fantasy. He would have liked to introduce in his family the custom of the father's blessing. Around Christmas, he had talked about it several times with Virginia; he had confided to her his wish that she would mention it to her sister and her brothers. He had given his beloved child an eloquent and enthusiastic description of the beauty of those family occasions in the old homestead at Saint-Michel. To make clear to her the richness of this venerable tradition, its supernatural atmosphere, the sacred character with which it had invested the authority of the father, he had known how to find convincing, solemn and gentle words.

On the morning of January first, Virginia, spontaneous and courageous as always, had kneeled before her father. Deliberately, in order to influence the others if she could, the valiant child had chosen her moment: breakfast-time, when the whole family was about to sit down at table, during the exchange of greetings and handshakes.

''Father, will you, if you please, bless me?'' Virginia had said, on her knees, her hands joined.

Lantagnac had raised his hands in the gesture of benediction. He had felt them heavy with all the sacred ministry of the patriarchs, his forbears. Deeply moved, to the point where the words almost stuck in his throat, he had placed his hands on his daughter's head, and slowly pronounced:

"Yes, my child, I will; but let God Himself, not I, bless you from heaven above."

Wolfred, Nellie and William were there. Respectfully they had watched the scene, no doubt secretly moved themselves. Not one of them had knelt.

Lantagnac, who on this day after Epiphany recalled the memory of that failure, no longer judged it with the same resignation. The theory of the iron wedge then came into his mind, with a new significance which terrified him.

"The iron wedge," he said to himself, "does not only penetrate into the soul itself. It strikes also between us; it is in the process of breaking up the unity of my family."

Did he know how close he was to the truth? Incidents were going to be piled on incidents to confirm his worst apprehensions.

A tradition of Loyola College called upon the students of the senior classes, each year, in the spring, to take part in an academic debate. Usually the students themselves chose the topic of the debate, subject to the approval of the dean of studies. Since the Ontario crisis the question of the so-called "national" schools had been the subject of heated public discussion. The young students of Loyola decided to make it the theme of their debate. The subject was therefore defined as follows: "Is it in the interest of Canada to adopt a single type of national school, implying the uniformity of programmes, textbooks, and laws on education?" It is not for us to describe here the dubious merchandise which is hidden in Canada under the high-sounding and deceptive label of "national school". In the minds of its promoters, a "national school" is little else than a non-sectarian, English school. Now, that year, William de Lantagnac was in his final year; he was one of the young speakers in the coming debate. Always defiant of authority, the young student proposed to argue for the affirmative. The dean vainly tried to point out to him the impropriety of such an action, and to recall the rôle being played by his father. William persisted. As the debate was in no way public, the fond hope was that nothing would go beyond the walls of the college. Silence seemed to be well kept on William's escapade; unfortunately, a trouble-maker had an account of the oratorical exercise published in an English newspaper in Montreal. The next day Lantagnac could read in the English press, in Ottawa, suitably alluring headlines: "William de Lantagnac, son of M. Jules de Lantagnac and a student at Loyola College in Montreal, upholds in a public debate the necessity of imposing on Canada the system of national schools." Needless to say, things did not stop there. The following day the same press set about exploiting the incident against the MP for Russell.

Lantagnac was most upset. The incident, insignificant in itself, assumed the proportions of a scandal. Public opinion was already placing the member for Russell among the leaders of the Ontario minority. At the congress of the French-Canadian Association of Ontario which had just ended, he had played a leading rôle. In the House, he never failed to protest against the slightest attacks levelled at the rights of the French language. Now the Loyola affair made two facts a matter of public knowledge: not only was the champion of French schools in Ontario sending his children to an English institution; but the MP for Russell was defending, against his opponents, opinions which he could not even get his own son to respect.

Lantagnac was deeply affected. The incident was distressing, less because it placed him in a false position with regard to his political opponents, than because of the painful impression and the feeling of disquiet that it would give his friends and all his persecuted compatriots. He who was uprightness itself appeared to his own people as a man whose

actions spoke differently from his words. What was he to do?
Deny the news? It was true, painfully true. The Rector of
Loyola had hastened to express his profound regrets to M. de
Lantagnac, without in any way concealing from him William's
rash behaviour. Besides, could the wretched father disown his
son, expose before the public the family reasons that had led
the young man to attend an English institution? He realized,
just from the nervous state of Maud and Nellie at the present
moment, that the least word from him might upset his home.
There was nothing for it but to swallow the indignity and to
grieve in silence. He resigned himself to it as best he could.
Solace came to him, however, from two sources at that bitter
time. Virginia, kind as always, soothed the paternal hurt with
hands even gentler than usual. Wolfred wrote a short note to
his father that read as follows:

My dear Father,

    You know what I think. However, I do not believe that
a son whose heart is in the right place and who has the
slightest notion of propriety should indulge in such
behaviour. I have written as such to William and I want
you to know.

                                        Your elder son,
                                        Wolfred.

[VII]

The Ontario school conflict was in its most acute period. The same hypocritical, harmful influences continued to be at work, in secret, against the French minority. Few days went by without new irritants being added to the old. In order to silence the Ottawa School Board, which refused to apply Regulation XVII, the provincial government did not shirk from violating the rights of parents. It declared dissolved the board elected by the taxpayers, and replaced it by one of its own, on which only one of the three members was a French Canadian. These arbitrary acts did not weaken the resistance of the persecuted. The "little board", as it was called by the populace, tried in vain to get possession of the schools. The children's mothers instituted themselves school guardians. Against this guard, the police proved helpless. The "little board" attempted enticement on the teachers. The attraction of large salaries was powerless against the disinterestedness of the brothers and sisters and the lay teachers. All of them, men and women, preferred to teach without a cent of reward, rather than submit to an iniquitous law. Unable to hold out any longer, the governmental board seized the school funds. Subjugated by starvation, the free schools were forced to close their doors; thousands of children were sent home to their parents.

The boys and girls did not waste their holiday time. Valour

and daring were the order of the day. While the little girls filed
into churches to pray for the salvation of the "Cause", the
young lads mobilized grocers' delivery carts, decked them
with flags and streamers bearing rousing captions, and paraded
through the streets of the capital. One day they walked up to
Parliament. Standing close together, under the falling snow,
the children waved their flags, and shouted at the top of their
voices: "We want the brothers and sisters." "We want our
teachers." "We want freedom." Passers-by stopped to watch
the demonstration. Some took off their hats and cheered;
others muttered oaths and denounced the tolerance of the
police towards such disorders.

Near the Victoria Museum, which had become temporarily
the seat of the Commons, two men watched the carts of the
young demonstrators passing by. The children's shouts rose
clear and shrill up towards Parliament. It seemed a quite futile
demonstration in face of this cold, grey, arrogant building, the
image of force holding rights in contempt. One of the two men
said to the other:

"You see, Lantagnac: today, those in power, behind those
walls, are scarcely disturbed. They act as if those shouts didn't
reach them. Patience, and you'll see. God willing — and He'll
do so sooner than people think — those children and their
cause will get their hearing in Parliament. And this will occur,
if only to teach the powerful that there are moral forces one
doesn't crush, even in this country."

The man who had just uttered these words had spoken with
extraordinary conviction. His person, his face especially, were
expressive of a contagious fighting spirit, a blend of good
nature, Gallic fire, and the exuberant valour of a musketeer.

"What do you mean, Genest?" — for the man who had just
spoken was in fact the chairman of the Ottawa School Board
— "what do you mean by a hearing?" asked the MP for
Russell.

"Oh! perhaps I spoke too soon," said the chairman,

smiling; "someone else will inform you. But it is well, I thought, that men like you should be warned, and should keep their powder dry. Don't forget."

He shook the MP's hand and was on his way. "What did he mean?" wondered Lantagnac again, as he returned to his chambers. He compared this statement with another made by Senator Landry, on the day the latter had asked him to stand for Russell. "The next act of the school tragedy will be performed in the federal Parliament," the senator had declared. Since that day, the MP had thought many times about that supreme occasion. At what time and in what form would it come? At first, Lantagnac had looked forward to it with joy, as a glorious opportunity to confess his patriotic faith and make reparation for his life's errors. Alas! his desire was no longer the same, now that the unhappiness in his home was making it clear to him how dangerous any great public action was.

Meanwhile the days went by; the end of April was approaching. In Parliament, the session was nearly over. It would not last beyond May. The leaders in the school struggle decided to hurry. One afternoon the president of the Education Association came into Lantagnac's office on Elgin Street. The senator was beaming. Without wasting a moment, he came straight to the point:

"You remember our last interview, Lantagnac. I had warned you that the crucial phase of the struggle would be played out in Parliament . . . Well, we've reached that point. I've seen Laurier, and he's agreeable. Ernest Lapointe will move the resolution; Paul-Emile Lamarche will speak also. Can they count on you?"

Lantagnac controlled himself as best he could. In a very offhand tone he asked:

"Do you expect much from this demonstration?"

"Much? That's perhaps overstating it. At least we expect something. In a constitutional country, as I don't need to remind you, one has to reckon with the power of public opinion. The debate will enlighten our enemies little or not at all; but transposed on to this wide stage the Ontario conflict inevitably becomes a national issue. The good will of Quebec will be strengthened by it; our people will draw some comfort from it. My dear Lantagnac, allow an old soldier to quote you an ancient axiom: 'In war, the most important thing is the morale of the troops.' And aren't the leaders those who create that morale?''

"No doubt," replied the MP, still on his guard. Then raising his voice, the better to control his emotion:

"My dear senator, you know my devotion to the French cause. You do me great honour as a neophyte. Allow me however to ask you for a few days to think it over. Perhaps you are not unaware of what's happening in my home. At present, I am not sole master of my decisions."

The senator got up to take his leave; he extended his hand to Lantagnac.

"My dear Lantagnac, I know, and I understand. Just remember that we value the support of your words a great deal; with them rest the strength and honour of our cause."

"Thank you," answered Lantagnac simply; "as soon as my reply is ready I shall bring it to you myself."

Towards the end of April it became known that Ernest Lapointe's resolution concerning the Ontario schools would be discussed in the House on May eleventh. Within twenty-four hours the news had spread across the country. On the list of speakers for this debate, everyone spontaneously put the name of the MP for Russell.

Lantagnac read the list in all the papers of the capital. Resigned though he was to there being some interest in his name, this noisy publicity none the less disturbed him profoundly. Even today, despite the trials of his life, Lantagnac cannot recall that first fortnight of May 1916 without feeling again the bitterness of a truly agonizing period.

During those long drawn out days of waiting, he was able to verify from experience how much more painful it often is to seek one's duty than to carry it out. What reply would he take to the senator? That was the obsessive question which continued to torture his mind. Would he take part in the debate? Would he choose to abstain? From either angle the problem that faced him bristled with thorny intricacies and tragic elements. To speak meant to reintroduce into his home the unrest of the election and perhaps to precipitate irrevocable actions between Maud and himself. How far would the underhanded manoeuvres of William Duffin not go, where his wife and children were concerned? The Irishman, whose devious activities were everywhere apparent in the school struggle, could not but dread a debate which threatened to clarify the responsibilities on both sides.

"Duffin," reflected Lantagnac, "will cause great trouble in my family; he knows that more than anybody I am aware of his scheming."

In addition, as Virginia had warned her father, the announcement of the coming debate, and the probable rôle of the MP for Russell, had produced much commotion in the Fletcher family. One morning just recently, no doubt after a bad night, old Davis had made a violent scene while eating his porridge. That morning he complained that the porridge was awful. Linking the ill humour of his stomach to the bad dreams of the night, old Davis had once more raised his hands to heaven and proclaimed the impending downfall of the Fletcher family:

"The government is tired," he had exclaimed with a groan, "tired of seeing that we let this Lantagnac carry on as he likes, and do nothing to stop him."

And the venerable accountant had added in a funereal tone:

"The minister has mentioned it to me, you know. That means that things aren't going very well for the Fletchers."

Then the old man had said, threateningly:

"We'll see however whether I'm master in my family."

Maud's attitude aroused the worst fears in Lantagnac. The first symptoms of a revival of racial feeling — which he had already noticed in her — were intensifying. He could no longer ignore them. Maud was not yielding solely to the urges of feminine despotism, any more than to the angry outbursts of her family or the insinuating proselytizing of Duffin; she was dominated and possessed by hard ethnic pride, the arrogant fanaticism which made her react aggressively against any manifestation of the French mentality. Only just recently, Lantagnac had been in a position to gauge the obstinacy of his wife. A new housemaid was about to be hired. Lantagnac had ventured to ask:

"Does she speak French?"

Maud's face had flushed scarlet, she had frowned, and retorted curtly:

"I thought, my friend, that those matters concerned me alone."

The housemaid had arrived the next day; she spoke only English.

After the thinly veiled threats that had abruptly ended their first interview, Lantagnac could no longer ignore the fact that Maud would be capable of going to any extreme. Would he dare speak on May eleventh? Once more his wife would consider herself misunderstood and provoked. It would mean perhaps their separation, and dividing the children between them, with the usual accompanying arguments and painful slights; it would also mean gossiping among the public, always eager to dress up family dramas with details of lurid passion.

"But then," went on Lantagnac, "must I abstain, and announce to Landry that I can't accept?"

He reflected immediately that abstention in such circumstances would be his political death, and death with dishonour. His solemn promise to the electors of Russell came back to him at every moment of the day: "If you send me to

Parliament," he had cried, "I pledge myself to one thing, and one thing only; but I stake my word on it as a man of honour: I will defend first and foremost your school rights." He recalled that he had carried this promise from one end of the riding to the other, and he had been elected, he was still aware of it, only because of that pledge. Could there be a more timely moment to redeem his word? . . . If he, the appointed defender of the Ontario minority in Parliament, kept silent, could one ask the others to speak? He remembered an incident an evening or two ago. He was returning home when he had met Sir Wilfrid Laurier, who lived near him, on the next street. The old Liberal leader had said to him, with his hand outstretched:

"Well, my dear Lantagnac, we are going to fight under the same flag! Believe me, I am highly honoured."

And the grand old man had gone on. That evening Lantagnac had mumbled some sort of reply or excuse, he knew not what. He had watched the olympian figure recede, already cheerless, like a tree losing its leaves. Each day was adding strength to the rumour that the desertion of the great man was about to be complete. It was said that all his English lieutenants were getting ready to betray him in order to rally to a union cabinet. And he himself, looking at his life now, from the extremes of misfortune, judged it severely, and sometimes, among his closest friends, even uttered the word failure. The sight of such a man, caught up again, towards the end of his life, in his French convictions, he, a man deemed, more than any others, responsible for the lethargy of his compatriots, stirred Lantagnac strangely, and made him ashamed of his own hesitations. Abstain? no, he could not, particularly after the Loyola incident. What would the French people of Ontario say? What would the whole of French Canada say? Would this not confirm the unfortunate suspicions which, as a result of that affair, he had not been able to hold in check? And what if the decent people, as well as all those who envied him, who were jealous of his standing and of the popularity which, although recent, was already considerable, were to say: "That Lantagnac is like all the others. He's a politician like the rest of them. He talks more than he acts"? The mere thought that his loyalty might be suspected brought a cold sweat to the brow of this proud and honourable man.

One afternoon when he was at home, ensconced in his study, considering the heart-rending alternative for the hundredth time, he heard the courtyard gate open and close. His study, situated on the second floor, looked on to the street. Through his window, he saw William Duffin, walking away, engrossed in his thoughts.

"Ah," he remarked to himself, "the brother-in-law's been scheming and plotting again."

Lantagnac was voicing more than a premonition. For some days Duffin and Maud had been seeing each other frequently. In a corner of the living room, they held protracted conversations. What plans, what new schemes did his brother-in-law have in mind now, Lantagnac wondered with a good deal of anxiety.

For some time, Duffin had been ingratiating himself to old Davis as Maud's supporter, and particularly as her advisor. In this capacity, he managed to make the Fletchers entrust him with a sort of supreme direction of the family's affairs. The officious Duffin had given his word, he had even pledged his reputation for cleverness: he would weave around Lantagnac such a network of subtle intrigues that he would prevent him from speaking on May eleventh, and perhaps even from appearing in the House. The moment having arrived to put the finishing touches on his schemes, Duffin had just come to see Maud. He thought Jules at his office, on Elgin Street. Maud had received him, as always, in the living room. Duffin, more insistent and obsequious than ever, began:

"Well, my poor dear, is there more hope today? Do you feel more cheerful?"

"Alas!" sighed Maud, very dejectedly, "very far from it. I am still wrestling with the same anxiety. Jules tells me nothing about his decision. I don't know what it is. For my part I don't dare broach the subject with him either. Yet here we are, the thirtieth of April; we have only twelve days left."

"So you think Jules is completely and finally won over to his new beliefs? No hope of a change of mind there?"

"Ah, my poor William, where have you been?" cried Maud, almost dumbfounded by the question. "Are you unaware of what Jules has become? Don't you know that he no longer goes to the Country Club or to play golf in Chelsea?"

"I know he has left the Knights of Columbus, and rather ostentatiously," recalled Duffin.

"Why," Maud went on, more and more distressed, "less than a week ago one of his old university friends, the lawyer André Raymond from Montreal, came here to visit him. This friend teased him a bit about what he called his 'conversion'. I listened to them talking, while I was explaining a page of Tennyson to Nellie. For you know that I understand French perfectly, even if I don't speak it much. What didn't Jules say? He described — that's not enough — he sang of his happiness, his 'gladness', at rediscovering, reconstituting his moral being. 'A feverish ambition grips me,' he went on, 'to reannex to my soul all the powers it had lost.'

'So you're changing your mind?' said his friend.

'More than that', he countered, 'I am making a revolution in my life. That is why I have never before been so inspired by French literature, French art, the history of France, and the history of Canada. In that atmosphere', he further confessed to his friend — here I recall very well his expressions and the enthusiastic tone of his voice — 'my faculties feel invigorated, fortified like a plant that has grown in a cellar and found the sun once more.' "

"But," said Duffin categorically, "that's pure mysticism! No, really, such a man is no longer amenable to persuasion by

means of reason. Only one resort remains to us, my dear sister:
to appeal to his pride and interest.''

''What do you mean?''

''This: you know that Jules is feared in high places. He has
talent, and something that is more rare: authority. I understand
that he would willingly be offered a 'sugarplum', as it's called,
a seat in the Senate, for instance, or an appointment to the
railways board, if only he would be accommodating, and more
discreet in his words and actions. Do you think he would be
open to such an arrangement?''

''Ah, Duffin,'' said Maud, shaking her head, ''I doubt it
absolutely. Don't you know Jules's intransigence? He has such
a haughty, unyielding character.''

Then, thinking better of it, she said with a touch of shame in
her voice:

''There's no reason however why you shouldn't try; we no
longer have the choice of our means.''

''And you know nothing at all about his decision?'' the
other insisted.

''Nothing at all.''

Duffin made as if to take his head in his hands, like a man in
a desperate situation:

''But after all, hasn't he any fear of the consequences of his
conduct and his obstinacy? What about his clients, the firm of
Aitkens Brothers? My information is that in those circles
people are very put out. To speak frankly, isn't he afraid that
certain influences may intervene, and force the Aitkens to
dismiss him?''

Maud made a gesture of discouragement:

''He ought to be afraid, certainly. We aren't rich, even if we
do live well. But he has such an independent character! You
know him: at the first attempt to 'force his hand', as he would
say, he would be the kind of man to throw his resignation in
their faces.''

Maud did not notice the gleam, the flash of covetousness

that showed in Duffin's eyes at that moment. Despite himself, her brother-in-law, too much on edge, had made a quick movement, as if, fascinated by some prey, he were about to dash forward with outstretched hands. Maud went on:

"However, I have a vague hope in that direction; I can't imagine that when he has thought it over he will want to expose his family to ruin for a motive of vanity."

"He must be earning there? . . ." asked Duffin.

"Twenty thousand dollars a year."

"Oh! the wretched man, and to risk such fees! Do you want me to talk to him, Maud? For after all, you know," he added in his most persuasive manner, "these are family matters. And to broach the subject with Jules, I should have to shelter behind you, to speak in your name. Do you want me to try?"

"Agreed," said Maud, not very confidently.

Duffin got up:

"Oh, in reality I've only a slender hope. But for you, Maud, and for your father who is so alarmed, I will see Jules. I'll try this final step. I'll use all my ability in talking to him. I will make him see the great man he could become tomorrow if he wanted to; I'll show him the danger of his life as a trouble-maker, the total eclipse he's headed for, and the risks to which he is leaving his family exposed. That's my part. You, Maud, following after me, you address yourself to his feelings; appeal to his heart as much as you can. Between us, God willing, we should achieve something."

"Oh! Lord, Lord!" cried Maud, bursting into tears. "How little hope I have! What an enigma I'm wrestling with!"

She sobbed for a few seconds, but quickly regained control of herself:

"All right, Duffin, go, and may God assist you!"

Her brother-in-law had left hurriedly. It was then that Lantagnac had noticed him going off, engrossed in his convoluted schemes.

"What has he just been plotting in my house, and where's

he off to at such speed?'' wondered Lantagnac, very annoyed by these clandestine visits.

William Duffin was heading straight to Rogerson, the cabinet minister, who was at the time the dispenser of high political patronage, a sinuous operator of consummate ability to whom the government was wont to leave the conduct of shady deals. Duffin, who knew his man, did not bother with diplomatic turns of phrase. Besides, this was not the first time he had come knocking on this door, through which he always passed, like a friend, without having to wait to be summoned.

''Well,'' said Duffin, as soon as he was in the minister's office, ''would you be interested, Rogerson, in keeping Lantagnac away from the debate on May eleventh?''

''Of course we would. Why ask me a question like that? Do you know a way?''

The minister leaned back in his chair, ready to do some hard bargaining over the deal; in his clean-shaven face, reminiscent of a Presbyterian parson, his eyes, like those of a wild animal lying in wait, suddenly grew intent.

''The way would be very simple,'' replied Duffin, ''and elegant at the same time, which is no disadvantage. You have a vacancy in the Senate. Promise me you'll offer the seat to Lantagnac.''

Rogerson's brow darkened:

''That would indeed not lack elegance. Only there is a small difficulty.''

''What is it?''

''The seat is already promised,'' said the minister casually.

''But a promise in only a promise.''

''No doubt, no doubt. If need be, I could see the prime minister and arrange matters. But first tell me, what hope do you have that the attempt will succeed with this Lantagnac? Isn't he very proud, very firm over principles?''

''Leave that to me,'' said Duffin, rubbing his hands. ''I know he's hesitating. He refused to allow the reporter from

The Citizen, whom I had myself sent expressly to see him, to write in the paper that he would speak for sure on May eleventh. Now a man who hesitates is a man one can tempt, isn't that so, Rogerson?''

''Only,'' Duffin went on, becoming very unctuous, ''as every labourer is worthy of his hire, I now ask something in return. That's only fair.''

And as Rogerson suddenly became pensive, the Irishman hastened to continue:

''Oh, have no fear, sir; I'm not asking for money, or a seat in the Senate. All I ask for is a word from you, and perhaps a little prompting.''

''Go on!'' Rogerson merely said.

''Well, now: Lantagnac, as you know, acts as legal counsel for the large firm of Aitkens Brothers. His earnings from that source amount, I'm told, to some twenty thousand dollars a year. Now I'm poor, Rogerson. The school struggle has taken much of my time, and deprived me of many of my clients, particularly among the French. Isn't it fair that I should receive compensation?''

''And you want Lantagnac's job?'' asked Rogerson, turning as if to resume his work.

''But supposing you arranged for him to lose it? And rather than leaving it to someone else . . .''

''Out of the question, my dear fellow,'' said the minister curtly. ''Do you suppose the man you are talking to hasn't thought before you of resorting to those means? The first concern of a good politician is to break the back of independents who become dangerous. So I've seen Aitkens Brothers. I have asked them to exercise pressure on their counsel, to lend a hand to the government. 'Impossible,' these gentlemen replied. 'Our clientele and our business require a bilingual lawyer; and he is a man of outstanding merit.' Aitkens Brothers, I know, will never dismiss Lantagnac.''

''Oh! wonderful,'' sneered Duffin at this point. ''Really,

Rogerson, it seems I can still teach a trick or two to an old pro like you. And that is extraordinarily flattering to my vanity,'' he added obsequiously. ''Who's talking of dismissing Lantagnac? My scheme is simpler still, and, I venture to say, more clever. If they refuse to give him notice, perhaps he may resign himself? What do you think? Supposing one approached this uncompromising character boldly, argued with him, even threatened him if necessary? After that, just let me know what you think of my method.''

Rogerson held out his hand to Duffin:

''Simply marvellous, my dear chap! When I leave the government, I'll name you as my successor.''

''Meanwhile, Lantagnac's twenty thousand dollars will suffice,'' replied Duffin, with a noisy laugh.

''But how will you get them? Having Lantagnac dismissed and substituting yourself for him appear to me two quite distinct operations.''

''Distinct, but linked. And here's where I have to ask you one last favour. Aitkens Brothers consider Lantagnac irreplaceable. It will be up to you, sir, to remind these gentlemen that William Duffin is also a bilingual lawyer, that he has a certain reputation, I believe, at the Ottawa bar, and that finally, if twenty thousand dollars is too much, I'm amenable to discussion.''

''All right, agreed! What a clear brain you have, my dear Duffin,'' said Rogerson pompously.

The Irishman then adopted his most conniving tone to add, before he left:

''Only, Rogerson, let there be no misunderstanding between us. I insist on it. I want only one thing after all: to rob the French cause of its strongest champion. To that end I am using a double-edged weapon. Nothing more. Tremendously proud men, as you well know, are more fascinated by honours than people think. Besides, I reflect that should the member for Russell be dismissed by Aitkens Brothers, he will be faced with ruin. Now, he has children. So, either ambition will make him agree to the Senate, or concern for his family will cause him to keep his fees. And there's my whole ploy. It is obvious of course, Rogerson, that I can agree to succeed Lantagnac only if he himself forces me to it by his obstinacy. For after all," concluded the Irishman, with the most visible sincerity, "I respect this man, who is worthy of esteem; above all I am very fond of his family, which is mine also. And his ruin would be the last thing in the world that I want."

"I understand, I understand," repeated Rogerson, who, however well accustomed as he was to vile behaviour, was none the less frankly revolted by hypocrisy of this kind. "Count on me, Duffin, I'll see to everything this very evening, and let you know."

He got up to intimate that the meeting was at an end.

The next day, May seventh, Lantagnac was kept at home by a slight indisposition. During the afternoon, having withdrawn to his study, the lawyer was resting quietly in his armchair, in a broad beam of sunlight that shone through the room. He was facing the window, watching the young maples nearby in the garden waving their branches, on which the first leaves were sprouting. They were unfurling in little cone-like shapes of a tender, young green colour, which seemed to be saying happily: how good the sun is! Lantagnac revelled in this springtime scenery, and recalled innocently his memories of a certain countryside. His thoughts were already floating far away yonder, over Saint-Michel, where these scenes of green rebirth possess such a striking beauty. Suddenly someone appeared at his door which had been left ajar: William Duffin was there in person. For some time the two men had been seeing each other only at occasional family gatherings. And even then Duffin, who feared the stinging banter of his brother-in-law, readily avoided him. Hence Lantagnac could not conceal a feeling of annoyed surprise. The mere sight of this cunning man was a cause of real physical suffering to

Lantagnac's frank and honourable nature. On his brother-in-law's lips was his most unctuous, florid smile.

"So," he began, pretending to joke, "all Irishmen are considered villains, incapable even of visiting an august invalid such as yourself?"

"You see, Duffin," retorted Lantagnac bitterly, "that's because I fear you less waging war than dispensing charity."

Duffin took or feigned to take this sally with good humour. He roared with laughter:

"I had indeed heard that you were feeling bilious today."

"And I am forced to tell you," retorted Lantagnac, "that your arrival has not made me feel any better."

The two men laughingly exchanged a few more gibes, then the conversation began to take a stormy turn. Besides, Lantagnac had forced Duffin to come straight to the point. Cutting short the visitor's preamble, he had asked him abruptly:

"Come, Duffin, now that you have fulfilled your charitable duty, what else brings you here?"

"Again charity, my dear fellow," replied Duffin, without being bothered. "You still intend to take part in the debate of May eleventh?"

"I still intend to do my duty," rejoined Lantagnac coldly.

Then Duffin put down his briefcase, which he had held till then under his arm. He set his pince-nez firmly in place, and assumed the appearance of a man about to wage a great battle. In his most patronizing and conciliatory tone, he set about developing some vague theory about the danger, for any minority, of resorting to uncompromising attitudes and to disruptive tactics. In that way one embittered the stronger party, which took a stiffer line and persisted in its injustice, when it would be so simple, so much more skilful, to argue matters, to win through cunning, "an honourable cunning," what one could not take by force. "Diplomacy is the weapon of the weak," repeated Duffin, harping on the same idea.

From there he went on to describe for Lantagnac the provincial government, tired, bored by this struggle, and wishing for peace provided it could be achieved without too much injury to the government's pride; the Irish element itself, assured Duffin, was only too ready to offer its hand to the French Canadians for the mutual defence of the Catholic schools in Ontario. In that direction, all they were waiting for was the chance of an honest understanding.

"Now you, Lantagnac, more than anybody else," concluded the Irishman, "are qualified, by your past and your prestige, to take on the superb rôle of peacemaker."

Lantagnac listened half absentmindedly to Duffin's homily, sometimes frowning, more often smiling. By way of reply, with a moderation that made his answer a scathing one, he merely stressed an obvious contradiction which had escaped his visitor:

"But how can you make out to us that disruption and intransigence are methods disastrous to minority causes, and on the other hand describe the government of Ontario, the persecutor, as bored by the struggle and ready to ask for peace? Tell me, my dear Duffin, how does your logic reconcile those two things?"

The objection visibly took the Irishman aback:

"Oh! I'll willingly concede you my theory. The fact remains: Toronto is getting tired, and it would be a smart thing to take advantage of that tiredness. Better still, my dear fellow;" — and here Duffin lowered his voice and adopted his most solemn tone — "better still I say, Ottawa is tired as well, it wants peace, and doesn't want this debate, which may spoil everything. There again, Lantagnac, people are counting on you. The belief is that you are the man to take this wretched question out of the political arena."

"And what then?" interjected Lantagnac, who was obviously getting impatient.

"What then?" resumed Duffin, whose voice became still

more gentle, "then, I am persuaded, or rather I am quite sure that the government would be prepared to honour in a splendid way the man who rendered his compatriots and his country such a service."

Lantagnac made a gesture of disgust.

"Come, my dear brother-in-law," the Irishman insisted gravely, "you entered political life to serve your people, I believe. Would an increase in honour and prestige which could reflect on your cause be such a criminal thing? So, be the great peacemaker the whole country is waiting for. Or failing that, don't appear in the House on May eleventh. Without your having to say a word or make a gesture you could become a senator, and perhaps something even better."

Lantagnac sat motionless, dumbfounded by so much ingenuity and low cunning. He got up. He pointed towards the wall, where on that afternoon the arms of the Lantagnacs gleamed in the sunlight. Above the crest of a count's coronet surmounted by a golden lion erect and holding a lance, he indicated the ancient motto of his family, standing out in sharp relief: "Rather honour than honours"; then, in a voice in which vibrated all the outraged dignity of a man of honour, he asked:

"In whose name do you come here, Duffin, and who do you think I am?"

And he stood waiting; there was a fixed, relentless stare in his eyes, trained like a trigger on his assailant's pince-nez. At that moment, the tempter's gaze became elusive, like his secret thoughts; his eyelids began to blink, to quiver, to beat quickly as if exposed to too intense a light; all of which did not prevent him from making a supreme effort not to lose countenance. He got up in his turn.

"Oh, sorry, Jules, sorry; I swear to you that I do not come in anybody's name; or rather I come in the name of your people. I give you my word that I have no other motive than to serve your interests and those of the common cause."

He gesticulated; his look had suddenly become firm again; his voice vibrated with sincerity, so much so that Lantagnac, still on the defensive, could not help admiring such perfection in play-acting and the art of simulation.

"One has to admit he's a consummate actor," he murmured to himself.

"For after all," Duffin went on, "where would be the harm if you accepted an appointment that gave you independence? Come now, Lantagnac, you're too intelligent not to look to the future. You're well aware that Aitkens Brothers may sometimes annoy you, make difficulties for you, hamper your political activity. I mention this because I know," he insinuated with an air of cunning.

"Enough, enough," broke in Lantagnac impatiently. "My dear Duffin, let's end this discussion. Know who I am, William. If I am made to choose between my fees and my conscience, then I shall opt for my conscience. But I shall not be the kind of man to be blackmailed, by you or by others."

And he motioned to the Irishman to withdraw. Duffin stammered a few empty excuses, picked up his briefcase, and left.

This interview took place on May second. The next day Duffin's plan continued to unfold mechanically. Summoned to the office of the head of the firm of Aitkens Brothers, Lantagnac had first to swallow a generous dose of advice about the good sense of moderation, and then a rather thinly veiled complaint as to the anxieties that the lawyer was causing his clients. There appeared to be some dissatisfaction in the Department of Public Works; there were signs of hesitation over the granting of new contracts. There was even talk of giving some of them to a rival firm.

"Oh, that's no problem," Lantagnac had replied curtly; "believe me, I'll see to it that those anxieties don't arise again."

That same evening, back at home, the lawyer, with a

cheerful and resolute heart, wrote out his resignation and had it
delivered immediately. The next day, he showed no surprise
when Virginia came to tell him:

"Well! Do you know?"

"What?"

"Haven't you read your *Citizen?*"

"Not yet."

"The name of your successor at Aitkens?"

"Who?"

"Guess."

"William Duffin."

"You've been told?"

"I'd guessed it the day before last."

He had not forgotten the very particular kind of aversion that
Duffin had awakened in him on his last visit. And the lawyer,
a well-read man, knew that as far back as the time of
Aeschylus treason was called "the foulest of diseases".

His resignation caused Lantagnac the loss of twenty
thousand dollars a year. He would not be ruined for all that. He
could hope that his clientele would gradually be built up again,
from among his compatriots. But for a few years he would
have to reduce his expenses markedly. This prospect did not
unduly perturb him personally, but it alarmed him greatly
when he thought of his wife. How would she accept what
would appear a debasement in the eyes of their society? And
since the resignation would have an impact on the children as
well, could Lantagnac defend his gesture against the reproach
of selfishness? Now, even more than at the time of the
election, he saw the urgency of explaining his conduct to
Maud. However, he postponed this explanation for two more
days. He might well feel strong before an assailant like Duffin;
but he recognized his weakness against the tears of a woman,
especially when that woman was the mother of his children,
the fiancée of his twenty-fifth year. Lantagnac was suddenly
delivered from all these hesitations. On the morning of May
fifth, Maud said, as she passed close to him:

"Lius, I want to see you in my room this evening, at seven thirty. Will you be free?"

"Certainly," said Jules, who could not help feeling momentarily shaken.

"Lius," Maud had said. She had just called him by the affectionate nickname, the abbreviation of Julius, which she had seemed to have forgotten a long time ago. This little word went straight to Lantagnac's heart. So Maud was going to bring all the power of feelings into play against him. He knew from experience how at certain times the Anglo-Saxon temperament is inclined to excessive outbursts of sentiment. Feelings that are too suppressed, kept too much in check by a severe upbringing and an excess of puritanical reserve, never stop half-way when they are given free rein. Lantagnac feared that in his wife's room, in the setting of their most complete intimacy, he would be dangerously weak.

That evening, at the appointed time, his courage recovered as best he could, he knocked on Maud's door. He found her sunk in an armchair. Another armchair was placed beside hers, to which she motioned her husband. Directly opposite him on the wall, during this long tête-à-tête, Lantagnac would have an old photograph, a distant memory of their honeymoon. Close by was prominently displayed a portrait of Maud, by Collins, which Jules had given her after Wolfred's birth, and in which she glowed with the full aura of motherhood. Here and there throughout the room were photographs of his children, artfully arranged by Maud so as to place her husband in an emotional environment. In a voice quivering with genuine affection she began:

"My dear Lius, you'll understand why I had you come here. Our intimacy has been dead for so long, through my fault perhaps still more than yours; I would so much like to see that, once back in its old setting, it could come to life again."

Lantagnac, expecting at least a few mild reproaches, felt somewhat disabled by this beginning. With a note of sadness in his voice also, he replied:

"My dear Maud, do you believe that I also don't regret what is lost, and that I would not be extremely happy to see all that revive?"

"Well, dear soul, I am willing to do all I can, to agree to any sacrifice, in order for that resurrection to take place. Are you ready to do as much?"

"But of course. How could I hesitate, Maud, to place our happiness and that of our home above all the sacrifices that honour does not forbid?"

"Very good," cried Madame de Lantagnac, somewhat reassured. "I recognize there your kind heart. But this evening I want to consider others than myself. I'm thinking, above all, of our children. You are not unaware, Lius, that your recent resignation affects them sorely. That's an income of twenty thousand dollars that they are being robbed of by our swindler brother-in-law."

"Since you judge that Duffin fellow as I do," observed Jules curtly, "his name shall never again be mentioned in this house."

Then, going on:

"But you don't mean to reproach me, I'm sure, with sacrificing our children for a selfish motive of vanity?"

"No," she hastened to rectify, "I only wonder whether you had the right to sacrifice them."

"I have done nothing but what I believed I had to do, be certain of that, Maud," he said, choking back an emotion that he felt invading him despite himself. "I thought, in all good faith, that the honour of the head of the family is property held in common, and that in defending it I was defending the property of all."

Maud sensed from the quiver in Jules's voice that his heart was beating more quickly. It was therefore in a still more entreating voice that she replied:

"But can I at least hope that this sacrifice will not be followed by any other?"

Lantagnac lowered his eyes and said slowly:

"Can I myself know where duty will lead me?"

He placed his hand on Maud's, which had come to rest on the arm of his chair, and very openly, with his usual nobility of mind, he outlined for her some of the lofty motives that would determine his coming decisions:

"I want you to know" he stressed, "that it is, without doubt, love for my nationality that presses me to action; it is also the dictates of my faith. You have very often confessed to me, Maud, how difficult it is for a convert to maintain his beliefs in a Protestant environment. You know, as I do, the terrible havoc which those same Protestant influences wreak in the Irish Catholic community. The newspapers and books that are read in those circles, the mixed marriages that are contracted there every day, work more effectively for heresy than all the preachers put together. Look at the heart-rending statistics concerning the pockets of Catholics which become Anglicized in Canada and the United States! You remember our frequent chats together about this sad subject. Now, if my compatriots become Anglicized, don't you think that the same destiny awaits their faith? Above all, let nobody raise against me the objection that in saying this I credit the faith of my own kind with very little solidity and very little resistance. Such objectors forget that at the present time Anglo-Saxonism is the most formidable force of all, that Anglo-Saxon literature is the all-powerful vehicle of Protestant thought, and that it will remain so for a long time to come. You know it, Maud, as I do, and you are grieved by it. But then I ask myself: who in this country, out of love for a false peace or ambition for a great political unity, who, I say, has the right to expose the faith of a whole people to the peril of death?"

Maud had listened attentively. Her faith, which had remained keen since the day of her conversion, fought strongly within her against her mind and her heart. She felt the power of the reasons put forward by her husband. However, quite determined not to give in, she ventured an objection that she believed supreme:

"I believe you are right in theory, and where your own people are concerned. But at the moment we are discussing mostly our own case, aren't we? And that of our children. We, my dear Jules, in our own environment, we have kept our faith; does it not appear that our children should keep theirs?"

"Will they all keep it, and for ever?" replied Lantagnac, speaking rather to himself, and staring fixedly at the wall, his mind contemplating a painful enigma. "Look at Wolfred and Nellie," he went on: "both of them are already threatening us with mixed marriages. What assures us then that their children will escape the common fate? Often, I confess to you, my dear Maud, this fear poisons my thoughts."

"But, dear man," retorted Maud a little sharply, goaded by the strength of the objections to be refuted, "would they have preserved their faith any better in your society of French-Canadian Catholics? I have occasionally heard you judge that society. Your judgements were very severe."

"Do I not know it? Catholicism confers no certificate of impeccability, my dear. But today we are speaking particularly of an atmosphere, aren't we? And so you will grant me this: true faith is more likely to survive where it is already in full possession, where it defends itself from behind the rampart of language, where it is enshrined in a collection of rites and traditions which, you will admit, have survived admirably among my people, so much so that the least conscious and least mindful families don't always manage to shake them off."

Maud uttered a long sigh. She had just experienced the weakness of her reasoning. But at the same time she felt surging within her a flood of feelings that would not give way, and were driving her violently to revolt.

"So, your mind is still set, and unrelenting towards me?"

Her voice softened on the last words, in fear of appearing a little sharp.

Lantagnac turned half-way round towards her; he looked at her for a few moments:

"How sad you seem, Maud. God knows however that only one duty divides us."

"But that duty you accept, my friend," she moaned, "even at the risk of destroying your home."

She let herself fall back into her chair, her head leaning towards her husband, and began to sob like a child. These sounds of distress, from a woman who was his wife, these sobs, in this room, completely upset Lantagnac. They awakened in his soul an echo of inexpressible sadness. He had taken Maud's hand in his, and, with his eyes lifted towards a photograph from their honeymoon period, he let his mind drift back to that distant memory. He could see once again a young couple, one May evening in the year 1893, walking along Dufferin Terrace in Québec city. Maud had herself chosen the Quebec capital for the end of their trip. That May evening, a band was playing national tunes on the terrace. Jules and Maud were lost in the throng of strollers, totally oblivious to everybody else. Maud was abandoning herself to the happiness of discovering her distinguished, handsome young husband. In this happiness was mingled for her the joy of her recent conversion, which produced in her soul a lilting gladness. He, isolated among his own people by his new convictions, was leaning on his young wife's arm as if it were the great and only support of his existence. He was walking along that evening, full of the double joy of having won his wife over from the Protestant faith and the superior race. The music from the bandstand gave wings to his dream. They walked up and down along the majestic terrace, from the dark escarpment of the citadel to the other end where, like gigantic silhouettes and emanations from an epic world, the belfries of the Upper Town stood erect in the darkness. Above their heads, in the atmosphere of a mild and mystic night, the stars merged with the glow from the Côte de Lévis and the moving lights of the ships in the roadstead, intermingling earth and heaven so intimately that the newlyweds no longer knew whether any earthly trace remained in their happiness.

Lantagnac pictured once more that Edenic scene of his youth. That it should come back to him at such a moment, in this room where his love appeared to be dying, brought tears to his eyes a well. Maud was still there, sunk in her chair, with her head resting on her breast, and sobbing desperately. She appeared to him to be in the deepest distress. He recalled the words they had exchanged during that unforgettable evening, on the terrace at Québec. He had said to her:

"You know, my blood relations are dead for me, Maud; you are my whole family and all my life."

She had replied:

"Jules, my conversion inevitably separates me from my own people. They tolerate it, but at bottom they do not forgive me for it. I have no one but you, but you will be everything for me."

At the memory of those mutual promises, the threat, albeit involuntary, that he was holding in suspense over his wife's head made him suffer a pang of remorse. He felt stirring in his heart a new sensation, one which he had dreaded when their disagreements had begun. Once Maud had become thoroughly unhappy, he was beginning to love her more deeply, not perhaps with the tender love that had enchanted the early days of their betrothal, but with an affection more disturbing to his resolve. He now loved her with a chivalrous kind of love made up of a deep pity for the weak woman before him, but more particularly of a determination to defend her against unhappiness. He leaned towards his sobbing wife. In his warmest voice he spoke to her:

"Maud, Maud, don't cry any more. Why this sorrow when you don't know yet what I shall do? I ought to have told you just now: I want to do my duty on May eleventh, but I don't know yet what it will command me to do. I have authorized nobody to say I would speak. Do you hear? Nobody."

Maud appeared to revive a little. Slowly she looked up at him, her eyes swollen with tears. And, in a voice still choked with sobs, she said:

"You do know, Jules, that I left everything for you. Don't you remember any more? No," she went on passionately, "no, I don't believe in duties which dictate such cruelties. You say, my dear, that you owe yourself to your people, your race, your blood. Do you forget that the same voice speaks to me and commands me?"

And not suspecting the awful gravity of the words she was uttering, so innate were her imperialist sentiments, she continued:

"It seems to you terrible that your children should be separated from their lineage? Do you not imagine that I suffer the same grief at seeing them break away from their mother? In me also the race instinct has awakened; it grips me and commands me imperiously."

Then, suddenly incensed, she added in a tone that was suddenly firm and almost harsh:

"Like you, I also can see all my own people behind me. I still have in my ears the terrible tone of voice in which my father said: 'Listen to me, my daughter: I gave your hand to M. de Lantagnac; but you recall what he was then, and what he wanted to continue to be. Rest assured, I won't allow Maud Fletcher to remain the wife of a French agitator.' And for myself I feel, and I warn you honestly, Jules, that if you were to become the public, acknowledged leader of revolt, there would be too much uneasiness, too many motives for discord between us, for life to be bearable for me here."

She ceased with these words, which issued painfully from her lips; she was aghast at the effect they had just produced on her husband. He had listened to her up to that point, leaning forward, his hands clasped, in an unconstrained manner. He suddenly drew himself up; his face assumed a firm, rigid expression which revealed an inner hurt, and the determination to defend his stand. Maud became afraid she had compromised everything. In her turn, she took her husband's hand, and, with impulsive tenderness, she said, seeking to look into his eyes:

"Jules, tell me that your duty won't command you to destroy me?"

She waited for the reply. Jules's features relaxed once more. Conquered once again by this fresh assault of a love pleading to be heard, he linked his free hand with those of Maud, and, giving them an affectionate squeeze, he replied:

"You well know that I wouldn't be as cruel as that."

[VIII]

Meanwhile, it was not without a good deal of anxiety that the federal cabinet was anticipating the debate of May eleventh. Nobody had any illusions as to the result of this parliamentary charade. The whole exercise would amount to an academic debate. The two camps would exchange salvoes of speeches; a few grenades would be launched, perhaps a few shells; then the vote would be taken and the Lapointe resolution rejected. The only worry was with regard to the leader of the Opposition. He would be speaking. His skill and his clever strategy gave rise to some apprehension. There was no lack of ministers or friends of the government who said: "Let us be on our guard. If that artful parliamentarian has decided to participate in the debate, it's because he expects an electoral gain." Some of the younger ministers, wiser than their older colleagues, were concerned about a more distant future. They could see a solid Quebec block gradually forming in Parliament. The school unrest in four of the provinces, and the too patent plans of the Anglicizers would, in their opinion, bring about the formation of such a block, which would eventually hold all governments at its mercy. Besides, however amoral politicians may be in their public life, they are not unaware of the persistent strength of moral ideas among the people. They know that persecution tactics become a dangerous game in the long run. Out of concern, or adroitness, they rarely omit to give their most infamous plans a façade of fairness. Perhaps more than elsewhere, these habits prevail in Houses inspired by the Anglo-Saxon mentality, a mentality which perpetuates in its parliamentary customs, just as in the old out-of-date ceremonies of this milieu, a kind of legal idealism or puritanical hypocrisy.

An anxiety just as great, although prompted by different motives, was prevalent among the leaders of the resistance in Ontario. One evening when Senator Landry was talking about it with Father Fabien, the senator had asked the Oblate:

"Have you any news of Lantagnac?"

"None; but I shall soon. I know he is to come today or tomorrow; he sent word by one of our Fathers."

"I am very much afraid of bad news," the senator had rejoined. "The Fletchers are raising an infernal hue and cry against our friend. His wife is involved, and frankly I think poor old Lantagnac is in a terrible dilemma."

Always confident, and from a need to believe in success, Father Fabien had immediately sought to reassure himself and to reassure the senator.

"Have no fear, Senator; the man who, in order to preserve his freedom of speech, has thrown his twenty thousand dollars back at Aitkens Brothers, will be quite capable of other sacrifices."

"Exactly," the senator had replied. "I wonder what one can still demand of a man who has just agreed to such a sacrifice. You will at least admit that it would be a great misfortune if the voice of French Ontario remained silent in this debate. Do you see the advantage that our enemies would not fail to derive from that silence? Lantagnac's abstention would also, I'm afraid, have a disastrous effect on our people. 'Why should we take so much trouble?' some would say, 'if the leaders don't risk their own skin?' In other words, Father," the senator had added, "I am worried about Lantagnac's political future. After the unfortunate incident at Loyola, may not his abstention authorize the worst suspicions about him?''

"Oh, that's something new!" Father Fabien had exclaimed; "the senator who now has gloomy thoughts!"

"Gloomy if you like, but realistic. Do you know that yesterday Lantagnac went to *Le Droit,* and asked that his name be omitted from the list of speakers for May eleventh? 'I don't say I won't speak,' he affirmed, 'but as a precautionary measure don't mention me.' ''

This time the priest's optimism had dropped slightly:

"If the MP for Russell has done that, it is certain that there are difficulties at home. He's not the kind of man to retreat."

There were indeed difficulties in Lantagnac's home. On the evening of May fifth, he had come away from his talk with Maud in total agony. The tragic words exchanged between himself and his wife during that hour had stirred the most sensitive fibres of his being. An unduly protracted nervous tension was robbing him of the usual control of his will; he felt it and deplored it. As in all cerebral types who have become so only through training, and through a lengthy repression of their emotional capabilities, there was in Lantagnac a tide of feeling just below the consciousness level which was always ready to overflow and engulf everything. What had become of that self-command which, in the worst setbacks of his life, had caused him to say with virile pride: "I am master of myself"? In this partial disarray, one prop remained to him: the rectitude of his conscience. His will was not assailed by selfish and vulgar motives. Temptation feels the need to cloak itself in the appearance of duty. He knew, for example, the weakness of the reasons Maud was putting forth against him. It would be so easy for the wife of Jules de Lantagnac not to share her husband's feelings — so absolute a concession, which he did not demand — but to accept them as the natural evolution of an honest personality, as the right of a conscience. How, in that case, could the husband of Maud Fletcher become a less worthy father, a less loving and loyal spouse, in practising the highest loyalty? Would he have dispossessed the mother in recovering his paternal rights? Lantagnac did not conceal from himself the extravagance of Maud's pretensions, based too exclusively on individual and ethnic pride. Yet it appeared to him contrary to uprightness, contrary to his pledges as a fiancé, to abandon after twenty-three years of marriage a woman whom he had drawn away from her family and from the faith of her forbears, and to do so after the solemn promise he had made to serve as her support in their stead. Despite himself a sentence of Maud's, barely modified, constantly resounded in his heart:

"No, it is not possible that duty can impose such cruelties!"

Lantagnac's perplexity increased with a strange intensity when he reflected that in his impending decision would be involved not only the fate of his marriage, but also that of his children, and of his very household.

"Are there then," he asked himself, without ever finding a decisive answer, "cases where the duty of public life can require such costly sacrifices?"

If, in his search for examples, he surveyed the spectacle of Canadian political life, he saw always and everywhere the rule, the total and universal triumph, of individual interest, often even of the most sordid passions. In that setting of cold reality his sacrifice, if he dared agree to it, looked like a naïve contribution to a gilded legend, something old-fashioned and almost laughable.

Reflections of another order, which at first he had refused to entertain, added to his hesitation. How, indeed, had the ideas of William Duffin, on the dangers of uncompromising methods in the battles waged by minorities, managed to find sanctuary in Lantagnac's mind? Lured by the need to fortify himself in his impulse to retreat, he had come to accept his brother-in-law's theories. No doubt he had been careful to cleanse them of 'Duffinism'; at least he flattered himself that he had. The essence of the doctrine was there, none the less, his mind, for all its nobility, was disturbed and almost won over by it.

One day, in the House, a young Anglo-Ontarian member who was very close to the administration, a man of moderate views and a friendly person, came and sat by Lantagnac.

"So," he said, "you'll be in this demonstration too?"

"Wouldn't it be my right and even my duty?" the MP for Russell replied.

"It's a great pity," the Ontarian rejoined, shaking his head with a vexed air. And he added, with apparent sincerity:

"Do you want to annoy the government? You'll certainly succeed. But allow me to tell you: this fracas will do no good either for your cause or for the country. You don't know, dear colleague, to what extent your friends are going to paralyze the sincere efforts of men of peace."

Thereupon the young MP had slipped away, leaving Lantagnac to his thoughts.

"Did that fellow come on his own initiative? Is he sincere? or is he some clandestine envoy of the government?" Lantagnac had wondered.

Such observations could not but strengthen his own doubts. Everything considered, he told himself, what had been gained in six years of struggle? The Ottawa School Board had lost one after the other, to a great extent at least, all the proceedings it had instituted for the recovery of its powers and its funds. It was clear that heavy weariness was daily overtaking the mass of the people, who were tired of fighting for no apparent gain. Besides, was there not a danger that this obstinate resistance would unleash a policy of reprisals? One could resign oneself to the fact that a large group, among the persecutors, would never disarm: the Orange faction, incapable of living on anything but hatred of the French and of the Catholics. In order to survive and maintain their resolve, did not these fanatics need disturbance and war, as a burning lamp needs air and oil?

More serious considerations arose in Lantagnac's mind. Had not excellent people, patriots whose sincerity could not be doubted, disapproved of the strategy of the leaders of French Ontario? The lawyer recalled certain distinguished deputations, whose mission had been to bring counsels of prudence and moderation to the oppressed. Had these prudent people been entirely wrong? Too hotly involved in the struggle, gauging men and events only through the dust of battle, had not the oppressed reason to fear for the accuracy of their judgement? In the beginning, perhaps, when a drowsy people had to be awakened to the imminence of the peril, the fight could be justified, it might even be necessary, as a strict duty; but after six years of these tactics, which had yielded what one might expect, was it not time to change one's weapons and one's strategy? At the very least, would it be so wrong to even try? Another temptation slid into Lantagnac's mind: if the day were to come when the rôle of pacifier would be vital, when the French cause might risk launching a timely diplomatic offensive, would not the MP for Russell be performing an act of wise patriotism by biding his time, by not giving the appearance of being a hard-liner?

For several days now Lantagnac had been feverishly turning over in his mind the cruel alternative. Hard days of exhausting anguish! Sometimes he would be tempted to examine himself, to wonder: "Is this really me? Am I not dreaming? Could I be, by some hallucination, the fatal hero of a terrible novel or drama?" At the moment when he believed he was strong in his conviction, completely reassured, doubt returned to him by a devious route, and tumbled the whole fabric of his fragile dialectics as though it were a castle built of cards. This man had for too long been in the habit of measuring each one of his acts by the rigorous rule of his reason and his faith. His conscience, unable to draw enlightenment from an irrefutable source, kept him wavering and uncertain. No doubt Father Fabien was still there; everything urged Lantagnac to go and see this wise counsellor. But some subtle, indefinable hesitation had made him postpone his visit to Hull indefinitely. In truth, he thought he could guess the priest's reply; he dreaded its strictness. Before facing this formidable adversary, he felt the need to consolidate his own position.

Hence it was still with hesitation, but armed from head to foot with the arguments he had been concocting for some days, that early in the afternoon of May tenth, the day before the debate, Lantagnac called on Father Fabien. The priest showed some surprise at the MP's visit: he did not attempt to hide it from him:

"Ah! it's you?"

"You were no longer expecting me, were you? I was wrong to send word too soon."

"To be quite frank with you," the priest went on, "I have been really sorry for you during the last few days. Not seeing you come, I said to myself: it's a pity, but he has dropped the idea of appearing in the House on the eleventh, after all. You are not unaware, I suppose, that that rumour is going around?"

"I was totally unaware of it," replied Lantagnac, a little surprised. "But frankly," he continued, "perhaps it is better that way."

And, with his hand pressed against his temple, he rested his elbow on a stool next to his armchair, and remained like that for some moments, his face contorted by an intense spiritual pain. Father Fabien looked at him in silence, strangely moved by the sight of this man who, strong as he was, now appeared crushed under the weight of his duty. Lantagnac was the first to speak:

"Father," he said, in a weary tone, "I have thought long and hard these last few days. I can tell you: I have been obsessed by the question before my conscience; and, to be honest, I believe it is insoluble."

Father Fabien asked him gently:

"Can one just ask how you state the case?"

Lantagnac settled himself back a little further in his chair.

"How I state it?" he began, his voice suddenly becoming firm again and clearly enunciating each phrase. "The first thing is that after six years of accumulated defeats I have no longer such a solid faith in our methods of combat. If I went into action tomorrow, I would go without enthusiasm. What's the good of hiding it from you? We are so few and so weak in Ontario. Our Irish brothers, I am willing to hope, will come back to us when the truth has enlightened them. But what's to be expected of the Orangemen? Will they ever relent, so long as we allow their leaders to keep their rôle as agitators, the rôle they thrive on? And so, quite sincerely, I ask myself this question: isn't it wiser to get by skilfulness and diplomacy what cannot be reconquered by force? Unless I'm mistaken, one extinguishes a fire by smothering it, not by stirring it up."

"Is that your whole difficulty?" asked Father Fabien, remaining calm.

"Oh no," Lantagnac hastened to reply, becoming more anxious. "The strategy which the leaders of the Ontario minority will adopt tomorrow strongly affects my case, and my own life. Understand me, Father Fabien: as your advocate behind the scenes of the diplomatic stage, Jules de Lantagnac can serve the Ontario cause to the utmost of his devotion, without disadvantage either for himself or for his family. But in the open fight and in the forefront, Jules de Lantagnac can serve, let's be frank about it, only at the risk of divorce or separation proceedings on the part of his wife."

Here Lantagnac paused, and looked for a moment straight at Father Fabien, whose brow became worried; then he continued:

"And so, I ask myself very seriously: have I the right, just for a move of doubtful effectiveness, have I the right to destroy my home, to bring about the dispersion of my children? I'll go further: do my duty as an MP and the devotion that I owe to my compatriots require such terrible sacrifices of me?"

"Indeed, my dear Lantagnac," said the priest in a deliberate manner, "your case is serious, very serious. What is worse is that it's the kind that can't be put before the public in order to justify an abstention."

After a moment's silence, the priest resumed:

"No doubt you expect from me a solution, or at least a few general directions? Shall we first, for the sake of clarity, take a closer look at the issues?"

"By all means," said Lantagnac, to whom the hope of an enlightened discussion restored some calm.

Then, between the two men, began a debate which was stern, closely argued, almost technical, but in which, because of the heavy stake involved, the verbal exchanges often assumed involuntarily the tone of tragedy.

"Well," the priest began, "the question before your conscience is twofold, or at least, unless I am wrong, raises two problems. First, you express doubt as to the effectiveness of an uncompromising struggle at the present time; secondly, you put before me your own particular case, the case of a father who very legitimately asks himself this question: should my devotion to the Ontario cause go to the limit of destroying my home? Isn't that it?"

Lantagnac nodded his agreement.

"So, let's tackle the first problem. And, if you will allow me, let us make a second distinction. To distinguish is to clarify. On the first point, my dear Lantagnac, you raise a question of fact and a question of principle, isn't that correct? You maintain that the method based on struggle has sufficiently demonstrated its ineffectiveness; furthermore you do not believe in the wisdom of that method as a means of defence for a minority. Once more, have I summed up accurately?"

Lantagnac agreed again.

"In that case, let us come right away to the question of principle. Once that is resolved, the question of fact will have a practical solution. Thus, Lantagnac, you reject battle, struggle, as a means of defence for an oppressed minority?''

"Reject them? Let us be clear to one another. Rather, I doubt their effectiveness. I believe that in this war as in any other, weakness can compensate for its deficiency only by skilfulness. In short, I don't think it is wise to rush head first against a wall.''

"You are partially right, my dear fellow," conceded the priest with a smile. "And in fact true doctrine, which is not so rigid as you imagine, reserves man's intelligence for less whimsical tasks.''

"But who then is right, the opportunists or the non-compromisers?" asked Lantagnac, with the anxiety of a man who saw his whole life hanging on the answer.

"Who is right?" replied the priest coldly; "neither of them. To rush forward is always unwise; to abstain permanently is inadmissible, not to say immoral. My friend, it is neither a matter of being opportunistic nor of being absolute; it is one of being prudent. Remember that word; it is the essential word. One of the rare pieces of good fortune that we Catholics have is to find in our principles enough to solve all problems, whatever they may be.''

"Oh, prudence! that's a word that in ordinary speech is strangely suggestive of opportunism!" Lantagnac could not refrain from observing.

"Wrongly so," retorted Father Fabien.

And the priest's face was suddenly illuminated, as if encompassed by the clarity of the exalted doctrine he was about to set forth.

"Lantagnac, your mind is accustomed to these problems; follow me carefully. Christian prudence, the queen of the moral virtues, is, as Catholic doctrine understands it, primarily an intellectual quality carried to a high degree of perfection. It is in the mind, how shall I put it? the great reflector which projects its light on all the actions of practical life. For any man who wants to act as a man, and still more as a Christian, must before everything else, as you will admit, refer his actions to the rule of truth. But, you will say, to apply that truth you must know it. Exactly. And here is where prudence intervenes, prudence which involves and supplies the knowledge of eternal principles. Think, indeed, how a man of prudence behaves: before acting he first makes a kind of spontaneous appeal to the principles of his faith, to the sovereign rules of moral philosophy. That is his initial gesture. But prudence does not live in the abstract. Its knowledge is a knowledge of application; to the knowledge of abstract and universal principles, it joins by its own virtue the tried knowledge of particular things. Good. Thus man is armed with the double knowledge of the abstract and of the practical. What then remains for him to do? He confronts the one with the other; he measures to what degree the universal principle applies to the particular object or action; then his conscience is flooded with light; all he has to do now is to obey the command of truth . . . You're smiling, Lantagnac?"

"With some reason! True, your doctrine, my dear Father, has a beautiful coherence; but it is strangely akin to that of the opportunists."

"You think so?"

"Absolutely. What do those gentlemen claim to do, if not to make adjustments between the absolute and the relative, the universal and the particular? Like you, my dear Father, they assert that a particular fact does not always permit of the application of universal truth. Therefore they sacrifice the latter to the 'contingencies', or, as they say also, to the exigencies of practical life."

"Correct, Lantagnac," Father Fabien retorted immediately; "they 'sacrifice' universal truth; and that is the unpardonable crime in their doctrine. What I maintain, as against them, is that prudence never sacrifices truth."

And the priest began to speak vehemently, as an inspired champion avenging stricken truth:

"No doubt," he said, "prudence is not absolutism, which

clings blindly to principle and scorns reality; still less is it opportunism, which scorns truth. For mark well, Lantagnac, when prudence moderates the application of the universal principle, it does so still by availing itself of the light given by this principle. Is this how opportunism, that intellectual scepticism, behaves? Quite the contrary, opportunists and liberals invoke only their own interests, their systematic fear of action and struggle, the so-called rights conferred by an excessive liberty, in order to sacrifice truth by abstaining from taking sides. For I ask you to mark well once more, my friend: it is again here that prudence is essentially distinct from opportunism. Prudence has no tendency to draw aside, to waver, to evade struggle and responsibility. Prudence, and I quote Aquinas himself, is a 'driving force'. You hear? A driving force! It is the light of the mind; when it has shown what duty requires, its principal act is to command action; this is what gives it moral perfection. So you see, Lantagnac, we are a long way from systematic abstention and conciliation.''

And, as the lawyer pursed his lips and looked a little sceptical:

''Oh! admittedly,'' continued the priest, ''prudence does not eliminate all obscurity in the mind, or all hesitation in the will. With it, one must still seek, ponder, above all pray, and exercise one's will. But it is true light and strength, which will always suffice for an honest man. How does it seem to you, my friend?''

''How does it seem to me?''

The MP appeared to reflect. Then he replied with an objection which assuredly, in other times, his forceful mind would not have entertained:

''It seems to me that your prudence, if I understand it right, will almost inevitably create non-compromisers and intractable agitators. In that case, I wonder what sort of answer you could give to people who said to you: 'Take heed, you who seek to fight; very serious reasons are required to disturb a country, a people or national entity. Social order must be safeguarded first and foremost. The weak or those in a minority must abdicate rather than compromise the superior good, which is peace.' ''

Father Fabien shrugged his shoulders:

''What answer would I give? The answer you gave yourself, Lantagnac, when you derived your principles from prudence. I should impose conditions and limits on agitation. It must have them. But once those reservations were made, I should say: 'Go, strike fairly, but strike firmly.' Then, I should ask in my turn in what way the defender of right is a disturber of the public peace any more than his offender. Is the citizen who shouts 'Fire!' in the street an enemy of law and order? Does the owner who drives away a thief with a stick unduly disturb social peace?''

This last rejoinder by Father Fabien seemed to impress Lantagnac.

''All the same,'' the latter said, ''haven't I the right to ask myself what your theory, as applied by our friends in the last six years, has brought them in the way of practical gains? As you know,'' he stressed, ''I am more than sceptical as to the results.''

''Good!'' said Father Fabien, drawing his hand once more across his brow. ''You bring me back to the question of fact. Let's examine it, in all sincerity, like the others. Do you want to?''

''What do you mean, do I want to!'' Lantagnac hastened to reply, in anxious haste.

''You say the method based on struggle has been ineffective? It avails nothing against the obstinacy of the persecutors? But why then those invitations to negotiate, which come to us from Toronto itself? Why are ministers here in Ottawa so afraid of tomorrow's debate? And is that all we have gained?''

''Ephemeral gains!'' interrupted Lantagnac, a little irritatedly. ''For after all isn't Regulation XVII still in effect?''

''What if it is?''

"But is there the slightest likelihood it will ever be revoked?"

"What does it matter if it isn't, so long as it's not observed? In fact, who in the French-Canadian schools of Ontario is concerned today with that iniquitous regulation? Yes or no, has French ever been taught more than in these recent times? Just listen to the complaints of the government's own inspectors: 'Regulation XVII,' they groan, 'embarrasses the bilingual schools; it is powerless to destroy them!' You know it, Lantagnac, as I do. Wherever it was necessary, wherever the Education Association has been able to make known its instructions, by order of the school commissioners the teachers have emptied their schools on the appearance of the government inspector. Elsewhere, small and poor school municipalities have courageously refused the Department of Education grants, in order to keep their freedom. But now I ask you this question in my turn: would our people have defied the law in this way, would they have spurned the money of the persecutors, if the clarion calls of the leaders, and the battle waged close by in Ottawa, had not revealed to them the sublime worth of what is in peril, and had not brought about an awakening of the national spirit?"

Father Fabien's voice had suddenly risen to the fighting, incisive eloquence which gave his listeners the impression of fencing with him. Lantagnac listened, certainly impressed, but still ready to take the offensive.

"I concede those gains," he said. "But need they be extolled so highly? Aren't they very precarious things? What shall we do tomorrow, when our people are tired and our resources exhausted, and the assailants return to the charge? For after all," he concluded emphatically, "the endurance of a people is a finite power: it has its limits."

This reply enabled the priest to give the discussion a still more serious turn:

"Yes," he went on rather solemnly, "yes, but the tenacity

of the persecutor has its limits also. As for that of the persecuted, let us not be too quick, I beg you, to say when it will reach the point of exhaustion. When a people is conscious of fighting for the highest essentials of its spiritual life, I believe in sources of energy beyond human conception. Lantagnac, remember that young sister, obliged to have surgery and refusing chloroform, because she wanted, she said, to offer up her suffering for the cause of the schools. Remember the story of that humble cleaning woman, returning one morning to the University to do her day's work, and first putting down in a corner the club with which she had done guard duty that night at the school in her district. Do I need to remind you again of the action of those unassuming fathers of Green Valley, disregarding a fine of five hundred dollars or six months in jail and housing their children in a wretched shed, in order to preserve the right to have catechism taught in French? After that, if you need to, look again at the legion of our religious brothers and sisters, the legion of our women teachers who have been working for three years without a cent of remuneration; count up the number of young teachers who barely a few months ago risked imprisonment in order to teach freely. Tell me, is there not, in these acts of devotion, the evidence of a people that will not be subjugated, the sign of a superhuman force that is supporting their courage?''

Lantagnac was too familiar with the stirring epic of those humble lives, he had too often praised it himself, not to be disturbed by this evocation. Yet his will resisted stubbornly, clinging as hard as it could to the last obstacles on the battle-field.

With his elbow on the arm of his chair, and his hand again pressed to his temple, he abandoned himself distractedly to thoughts that led nowhere. In his soul the same anguish still persisted. Or rather it had gone on growing, in proportion as the shaky supports on which he was trying to ground his conviction had collapsed. As the light grew clearer in his mind, the more urgent summons of duty increased the revolt of his sensitivity. A prey to the most intense agitation, he got up and began to walk up and down in the priest's cell.

"So," he sighed "if you are right as opposed to me, Father Fabien, if the plan of the leaders is the right one, all I can do is conform to it; and I must do so at the price of my happiness, even at the price of my home?"

The priest looked at the lawyer for a moment, noting how his features were altered by distress. He realized the cruel seriousness of his rôle as a counsellor. He cast about in his mind for less rigorous formulae, for all the palliatives that doctrine could permit.

"Lantagnac," he began, "aren't you afraid of adding unduly to the already tragic nature of the problem? Have I ever mentioned that your sacrifice should go so far as to turn you into the destroyer of your home?"

"But isn't that what all my friends ask of me, demand of me?" retorted the lawyer, walking over to his armchair and leaning against its back, with a bitter grimace on his lips.

"Not as far as I know," corrected the priest. "Many are unaware of the cruel alternative you are wrestling with. Those who have come to know of it pity you, my poor friend; but among them not one, I assure you, dares to require such a sacrifice from you."

"But you, Father, what do you say? Have I the right to sacrifice my family, my children, for the benefit that the Ontario cause will derive from tomorrow's debate? Have I the right?" repeated Lantagnac, whose eyes involuntarily assumed an expression of defiance.

"Have I the right? Have I the duty, you mean," rectified the priest again, speaking gently. "At this point, my friend, allow me to state the principle to you, then leave you to draw the conclusion. Your case, Lantagnac, comes under what we call in ethics — allow me an expression from scholastic philosophy — the 'indirect will'. If you speak tomorrow, you perform an act from which a bad effect may result, but also a good. Are there sufficient reasons for performing that act? Does the good effect that we hope from it justify you, even order you to act, without our taking into account the unhappiness which may indirectly follow from it? There is the whole problem.''

''But then,'' replied the lawyer, who was growing paler, ''to speak tomorrow is to perform the act of breaking with my wife. Have I the right to perform that act?''

''The act of breaking, you say?'' queried Father Fabien once more. ''Who will perform it, you or Madame de Lantagnac? No, my friend, the act of breaking, it is not you that will perform it, but the volition of your wife, and it will be an improper act. Your own act is an act of duty, an act to which you are perhaps forced by your commitments as a public person, your obligations as a member of Parliament. That is your act.''

''But is it not self-evident that the break between us will inevitably follow action, as the consequence follows its cause?'' insisted Lantagnac, who grew more and more pale and nervous. ''In that case, I want to know, is there a serious, an urgent reason to re-examine the cause? Father Fabien, I ask you once again: will this debate count so heavily for the future of the French schools in Ontario that I, Jules de Lantagnac, must accept the rôle of a martyr?''

There was a feverish glitter in his eyes. But already, in a ringing, confident voice, which revealed the firm control that his will was rapidly assuming over his feelings, he added with dignity:

''Note, Father Fabien, that if I refuse to bear the remorse of having destroyed my family, I do not want either to bear that of having betrayed my duty. I want to accomplish one thing, one only: what is commanded by my conscience. But I request to be told what it is.''

''Once again, my friend,'' continued the priest gently, ''it is a problem that I hesitate to settle, that I would have preferred to see you settle yourself.''

Father Fabien gave a half turn to his chair, as if he had

wanted to avoid a decision. Then he swung his chair back, and with his eyes looking directly into those of his spiritual charge, he continued:

"My friend, there is a conflict here between two obligations; I am seeking which one must prevail. A duty of charity and also of social justice binds you undeniably to your family. A duty of charity and also of social justice binds you in the same way to your compatriots, in your capacity as an MP. In certain respects, this debate of May eleventh is only one demonstration, more solemn than others, an important offensive, but one which will not end the war. And certainly, from that point of view, nothing is grave enough to require from you an intervention with such cruel consequences. On the other hand, may or may not the abstention of the MP for Russell compromise the final outcome of the war? That is the real crux of the matter. It crosses my mind that, in the eyes of a public too ill-informed of many circumstances, and following the incident involving his son William at Loyola, Jules de Lantagnac cannot keep silence tomorrow without dishonouring himself for ever, and without destroying the prestige of a great talent. That being so, has he the right, he, a leader invested in the eyes of his own people with a kind of moral sovereignty, has he the right to annihilate the influence for good that he can exert? I reflect further that for the mass of this poor people which has been struggling so painfully for six years, his abstention can only be a subject of scandal and a temptation to defeatism. Oh! I can hear all too well the sad cry that will echo tomorrow almost everywhere in Ontario and throughout all French Canada . . ."

And here Father Fabien, looking towards the window, towards the Ontario countryside, seemed to be sweeping his eyes over the suffering and persecuted multitude: ". . . I hear all too clearly the weary lament of those poor victims: 'Another leader who is abandoning us!' they will exclaim. And I'm afraid, Lantagnac, I can't hide it from you, that the people, feeling itself abandoned by its leaders, will abandon everything itself. At the time I am speaking to you, the task of the dominant figures of our people seems to me to be of a very special and imperious nature. The upper classes have been found wanting for so long. If the leaders, the great men, do not rehabilitate themselves by offering the example of some exalted sacrifice, how do you expect the lesser men not to say to themselves in the end: 'But is it always up to us to pay, to sacrifice ourselves, to give our sweat? Always up to us to till fresh ground, to have children, to supply priests and sisters, to preserve morality, and life itself?' ''

The priest paused for a long time. He seemed to be meditating. Then, in his grave voice, he slowly concluded:

"So, my friend, everything being weighed before God, you see where my decision leans."

"Thank you, Father," Lantagnac replied simply, his eyes red with tears.

He took a few steps in the room and said:

"Forgive me however if I still hesitate, if I don't dare to say to you that my internal struggle is over. I am a husband and a father."

And he went back and leaned on the back of the armchair, his face buried in his hands, as he made a superhuman effort to keep his feelings under control. Father Fabien himself could hardly contain his emotion. In one of those simple gestures of faith that came spontaneously to him, he took his crucifix in his hands, knelt, and prayed for a few moments:

"Oh Jesus burdened with the cross," he entreated in a subdued voice, "give light and courage to this soul in distress."

The priest's adjuration made Lantagnac draw himself up. Father Fabien had risen to his feet. Turned towards his spiritual charge, he now said to him, in a voice charged with the greatest indulgence:

"My friend, if only you knew how I understand your

heartbreak. Few men in this life are confronted by a duty beset with such tragic difficulties. At this hour, however, I can divine that more than the concern for your tranquillity and your happiness, one thought weighs you down: that of your children. Still more than their French soul, you want to save their Catholic faith. Tomorrow, Lantagnac, if as I hope you decide for heroism, remember the recommendation I make to you: do not fail to offer up your sacrifice for your children.''

And the priest added in an inspired tone:

''My friend, the greatest service one can render to a cause is still to suffer supernaturally for it.''

Lantagnac fell to his knees in his turn.

''Father, bless me and pray hard for me. For myself, I am going to think and pray a great deal more.''

Lantagnac went back towards Ottawa taking with him the same tormented mind. Some light had come to him. He felt liberated from Duffin's sophistry. But the decision, the solemn decision which tomorrow the MP for Russell would ask of Jules de Lantagnac, that he had not yet taken. And he realized that the emotional tension that gripped him deprived him too completely of his serenity of judgement and of his self-possession for him to be able to take it.

As soon as he had stepped on to the interprovincial bridge, he felt a little calm return to him. In front of him, at the top of Nepean Point, the Sieur de Champlain stood proudly against the clear May sky, still on his way, with the same step, towards heroic adventures. A kind of joyous vibration rippled through the air: the gaiety of things singing their joy as they returned to life after the long winter torpor. All the vast, murmuring resurrection of Canadian nature was singing its Alleluia. Yonder, towards Quebec, the last wilted traces of the previous autumn were disappearing from the face of the Laurentians, under the burgeoning hope of new greenery to come. On the Ottawa river, tiny pieces of snow and ice, which had come from the banks where the shade of the firs and the dark pines had preserved them, glided gently downstream, like flakes of foam. The warm spring breeze brushed Lantagnac's face, bringing to him a breath of youth and vigour. The breeze came from the capital; but it seemed to have passed over the town without touching it. Gentle and soothing, it now crossed the river, heavy with the smells of distant fields, the scents of greenery, still young, and of the first buds that had burst in the short grass and the new forests, the early flowering of the maples and willows, the elder-blossoms in their white fur, the fresh aroma of soil delivered of frost and steaming once more under the prongs of the sowers and the harrows. The breeze which softly wafted over the tired face of Lantagnac made him want to extend his walk. He looked at his watch.

"Already half-past four! Too late now to go to my chambers. I'll walk a bit and meditate to relax."

He turned off through Major's Hill Park, passed by the high turrets of the Château Laurier, and headed towards the Parliament buildings. Since the mysterious fire of February third, he had not returned to the site of the disaster. He climbed the second slope of the broad esplanades, from where he could see the ruins at a glance. What a frightful sight! Where scarcely a few months before, the parliamentary tower and the vast English Gothic buildings had stood, nothing remained but a chaotic mass, vaults and walls that had caved in, windows staring eyeless from crumbled, blackened sections of brick. Here and there charred beams were left suspended, dangling like arms of skeletons; at the summit of the tottering walls, large iron sheets moved and creaked in the wind, sounding like ill-omened birds calling across this scene of devastation. Lantagnac's eyes ran over this sinister landscape from one end to the other. Suddenly his emotion became intense. At each extremity of this field of desolation, he had just perceived, still standing on their pedestals and seeming to be meditating on the disaster, two lines of men of bronze. He recognized them and named them: Georges-Etienne Cartier, Alexandre Mackenzie, George Brown, John-A. MacDonald . . .*

These statues, still there in solitude before the pile of rubble, cast a kind of Aeschylian melancholy over the scene. The MP knew: the collapse of the Parliament buildings had, in time, taken on a symbolic value. Several people had not been able to help seeing in this, in the fierce clash of nationalities, at the height of the battle, a premonition of the destruction of Confederation. Absorbed in this thought, Lantagnac looked round again at the statued figures. They gave him the impression that they were meditating on a political and moral downfall more lamentable than the ruins piled under their eyes.

And Lantagnac came back to the doctrine of Father Fabien, whose clear wisdom was illuminated before his eyes:

"What an impressive object lesson! Those who fight for the respect of justice and right are called agitators, sowers of discord, demolishers. And that's that! This country is dying because the concept of right is already dead."

Turning left, he set off to walk round the ruins. A crowd of workmen was busy clearing the ground. The stroller circled the rotunda of the library, the only portion of the historic building spared by the fire. He came out on the right side. Near the Baldwin-LaFontaine monument, on the edge of the parapet, a group of young people were talking and gesticulating excitedly. By their velvet berets he saw that they were students from the French university in Montreal, who were no doubt on a trip to Ottawa. As Lantagnac came up, the group moved away. Only two students remained behind, continuing to chat as they looked at the monument in profile. One of them said, clearly enough for the MP to hear:

"This is the statue, you remember, that our friend Wolfred Lantagnac advised us to go and see."

---

*Spelling as in Groulx's original. (Translator's note)

"That's the one," said the second.

"One has to admit, the sculpture does embody an idea."

"Yes, particularly for a fellow like Lantagnac, who's so obsessed by problems of national identity."

"Yes, obsessed is the word."

The stroller stopped, riveted to the spot by these last words and by the name of Wolfred. What were those students telling him? Was a drama similar to his own being played out in the soul of his eldest son? The father would have given much to learn more at that moment. He listened intently. The two students hurried off, summoned by their friends.

Lantagnac lingered also before the sculpture. In the obsession that possessed his mind, the monument assumed a strange vitality. The two bronze figures stood erect on their hemicyclical pedestal of white granite. Both of them were tall, very dignified in their bearing, with well proportioned heads and firmly set shoulders; by their very attitude, as they stood facing each other, they evoked that moment of history when the two national groups had learned to make peace while respecting their mutual equality to the full. The artist, as we know, has represented the twin architects of Canadian freedom at the solemn moment when the two, both of them leaders of their nation and of their province, discussed the alliance of 1840. Baldwin, his head bent a little forward and his left hand resting against his frock-coat at chest height, is reading a parchment. He is a man who is openly presenting the clauses of a contract. LaFontaine is listening, standing very erect, with his right hand supported on the pedestal, his left hand on his waist. Here is depicted neither a conqueror nor one who is vanquished, neither a superior race nor an inferior one. Equal is treating with equal. The two men are on the same footing. And Lantagnac thought he could hear the French-Canadian statesman conveying to him by his whole bearing, as he had formerly proclaimed them in his speeches, the words:

"I ask for my province and for my compatriots an equal

share of rights, power, and honours. Nothing more but nothing less.''

Lantagnac started on his way home, with this great lesson of courage and politics echoing in his ears. For the future leader, the light of victory had not yet shone. A little serenity seemed to have descended upon him. As he was crossing Connaught Square to enter Rideau Street, a figure suddenly appeared that almost stopped him in his tracks. From a distance of some hundred yards, his briefcase under his arm, his brother-in-law William Duffin was approaching. The new lawyer for Aitkens Brothers was wearing a straw hat of the latest fashion and an expensive grey suit, such as he had never been known to wear before. Quite resolved to pass with his head held high, Lantagnac could not help wondering:

"Will he dare greet me?"

Duffin, who was walking briskly, at first appeared put out by this unexpected encounter. But, always brazen, he raised his hat in a friendly gesture and remarked slyly to his brother-in-law:

"Excellent news, my friend; the papers are saying you won't speak. My hearty congratulations.''

Lantagnac started under the lash of these compliments, which were like the most insolent of affronts cast full in his face. For a moment he looked haughtily at the passer-by; then he continued on his way in a dignified manner, without uttering a word, but mortally wounded. A few steps farther on, he stopped a little newspaper vendor. A glance at *Le Droit* gave him the information:

"M. de Lantagnac, prevented at the last moment by grave reasons, will be unable to take part in the parliamentary debate on the bilingual question.''

"Our friends,'' he said to himself, "are taking precautions against the scandal of my abstention. They're preparing their public.''

He arrived home, more upset than ever.

[IX]

On that morning of May eleventh, long lines of children filled
Chapel Street, from York Street to St. Patrick, as they moved
towards Saint Anne's Church. Little girls, wearing their first
communion dresses, advanced slowly, like a trail of white silk
barely fluttering in the wind and broken at intervals by the
black veils and brown habits of the Sisters. Then came the
stream of little boys, more restless and talkative, led by
Brothers wearing white bands and broad felt hats. From their
doorsteps, a few simple folk watched the vibrant procession go
by.

"Where are the schoolchildren off to this morning?" the
lady grocer asked the milkman, whose cart was held up by the
dense little crowd.

"Don't you know?" replied the other. "Today's the day of
the great speeches in the House, in favour of our schools. One
has to pray a bit so that things go well."

"Why, so it is!" said the grocer. "Tell me, there must be a
few of your own in that crowd?"

"Six of them," said the milkman, proudly: "four boys and
two girls. But there are others at home. It's as they say,
Madame: you don't have to press the little ones these days to
pray for their schools."

"Ah, yes," exclaimed the woman sententiously: "the

young ones growing up today will deserve better treatment than we got.''

"You know, it would be really an interesting thing,'' said the milkman, warming to the subject, "to count the rosaries and Ways of the Cross that my little girls have said this winter and spring. And all that — that's the fine thing about it, Madame — just so we can keep our language in our schools.''

"Yes, that's the fine thing about it,'' echoed the woman.

"You remember, the boys went off one day in carts right to the door of Parliament, to heckle the ministers: Naturally the little girls couldn't take part in such a racket. They helped by going to church instead. One day I said to myself: 'I've got to know more about this!' So I asked my Germaine, a wee bit of a thing, about that tall, dear lady, and barely nine years old: 'Well now, what did you do at church today, dear child?' ''

" 'I did an hour of adoration, papa,' she replied.''

" 'An hour of adoration!' I said. 'But didn't you find that too long, a little tot like you?' ''

" 'Too long!' she came back with; 'would you believe I forgot myself and stayed there an hour and a half?' ''

"Ah, the dear child!'' exclaimed the grocer again. "What a fine action, for God's sake!''

"All the same, it's a great pity,'' added the milkman, in another tone. "Did you see the bad news in the papers yesterday?''

"No, I didn't. Bad news?''

"You didn't see that M. de Lantagnac won't speak in the House this afternoon?''

"M. de Lantagnac, that fine tall gentleman who spoke this winter, in the basement of Sacré-Coeur Church? The one who speaks so well?''

"Exactly.''

"But why?''

"Apparently there are obstacles in his way!''

- - - - - - - - - -

A man who also had been waiting until the sidewalk was clear of the stream of children was able to hear the latter part of this exchange. He stood there, very dignified in his top hat and frock-coat, holding his prayer book, a young girl on his arm. Suddenly, as a squad of children went by, whether in a spontaneous gesture or the result of prompting from the Brothers, forty caps were raised, and young vibrant voices began to shout: "Long live M. de Lantagnac!"

Lantagnac, for it was he, acknowledged the greeting with emotion.

During the night that had just passed, he had reflected more than he had slept. Moreover, a fright had kept him and his family up until late in the evening. Almost immediately after dinner, Maud had fainted. Hastily called in, the doctor had diagnosed a passing nervous upset, the result of over-exertion, and had advised change and rest. Up early the next morning, Lantagnac had recalled that a Mass and children's communion was being held at Saint Anne's Church for the success of the great debate. He had decided to go. Incapable of helping any other way, he wanted at least to go and pray for the oppressed, to join his voice to the all-powerful supplication of the children. Virginia had naturally accompanied her father, and it was she to whom he now offered his arm, she to whom he had just said, as the children filed by:

"Our enemies don't know what power we are lining up against them this morning."

Lantagnac, a man of strong and deep faith, was aware that he was not uttering empty words. And as Virginia had just recounted how at a certain gathering the day before, where today's ceremony had been mentioned, a number of people had ventured to judge these children's demonstrations unnecessary, verging even on rowdiness:

"Ah, those armchair Catholics!" he had protested. "Always the same!"

And he had made a statement that accurately conveyed the religious loyalty of his spirit:

"My child, there is for me one fault worse than that of the unbelievers: that of believers who do not follow their faith to the end."

When the crowd of children had entered and filled the church, Mass began. Slowly it unfolded in the very simple, old church, whose only adornment that morning was that of the solemnity of souls. After reading the gospel, the celebrant turned his back to the altar for a moment. In a few words, he reminded the young congregation of the intention of their prayers and communions:

"Children," he said briefly, "it is for your schools that you have come to pray and receive communion this morning. Remember that great intention. This afternoon your schools will be discussed in the federal Parliament. You will ask God, particularly in a few moments, when He will be with you, you will ask Him to enlighten and sustain our defenders, to inspire them with the words that befit our cause. You will ask Him also to open the eyes of those who do us ill, who want to take from you the good Brothers and Sisters, those who would like to prevent you, little French-Canadian boys, and you little French-Canadian girls, from learning your mothers' language."

Mass continued. On the wooden pews, rosaries clicked, or moved feverishly between little fingers; from human lips rose a murmur that filled the church. At the offertory, the congregation of children responded with one accord to the martial challenge of the canticle:

"We want God, He is our Father,

We want God, He is our King!

We want God in our families . . .

We want God in our schools . . ."

Kneeling in one of the last pews, at the back of the church, Jules de Lantagnac prayed fervently. Just before, with the brief words of the priest uttered after the gospel, something had stirred in his heart. Once again he found himself envying the fate of his colleagues in the House, who with more freedom than he had would have the honour of serving the cause of justice. His emotion had further increased when beside him Virginia's voice, mingled with that of the children, had begun to sing freely:

"We want God, He is our Father,

We want God, He is our King!"

Then came the communion, the long lines of white veils and young bowed heads moving down the aisles towards the ciboria which were being carried back and forth. When the last communicants were about to leave the altar rail, Jules de Lantagnac and his daughter came up in their turn. With a grave, meditative air, they returned to their seat, feeling the eyes of those thousands of children, dimmed at that moment by an intense emotion, directed towards them.

Mass concluded. The celebrant, kneeling at the foot of the altar, recited aloud the prayer of the little Ontarians to Joan of Arc, a prayer to which Pius X had one day given his august blessing with these words, written in his own hand: "We hope that this prayer may rapidly obtain what it asks."

"O, Christ, friend of the Francs!" began the priest, and the congregation continued, the sound swelling and reechoing through the church: "You who, by the arm of a humble virgin, once saved France, incline towards us the great mercy of your Sacred Heart. We entreat you through the merits and intercession of the Blessed Joan of Arc, whom we choose as our patron saint, protect our institutions, our language and our Faith.

O Christ our King, we swear to you eternal loyalty! Grant that nourished with the bread of your Holy Eucharist we may grow into a perfect people, and that we may be worthy to continue in this land of America the glorious traditions of the eldest Daughter of the Church.

O God of Joan of Arc, save France once more! Save our dear Canada; and you, Blessed Joan of Arc, pray for us. Amen.''

The church emptied, as the same voices carried out into the street the refrain that gave expression to the fervent courage of this fighting youth:

"Never, never shall they have it!

Never, never shall they have it!

The soul of New France.

Let's raise once more this valiant cry:

Never, never shall they have it.''

Lantagnac and Virginia were the last to leave. Virginia, still singing with the children, leaned more affectionately against her father. Lantagnac, his eyes a little moist, felt his anxieties of the last few days returning. In the morning, he had got up resolved not to speak. Seeing the happiness which had overtaken Maud the previous evening, after the news had appeared in the papers, he had begun to make up his mind.

"Obviously," Madame de Lantagnac had said to herself, "that announcement could have appeared only with Jules's authorization. So, thank God, we are spared the great disaster."

Then, when suddenly he had noticed Maud slumped in her chair, and once the doctor had spoken, Lantagnac had refused to allow himself to reawaken her apprehensions. He had believed his moral dilemma settled by this incident, and had resigned himself to the fact. Moreover, a subtle illusion, well calculated to deceive a lofty spirit, was then dominating his thoughts. He had said to himself:

"To speak will mean honour for me; to abstain, dishonour. If I accept humiliation for the cause, will not this sacrifice serve it more effectively than my words?"

That was where he stood when he had entered the church. When he came out, his resolution no longer appeared as firm to him. The sight of that assembly of children, almost a generation, who might tomorrow be perverted by Anglicization, had revived his fears. He was afraid of the future, afraid of not doing, in order to save that generation, all that duty might require of a man of faith. Then he thought of all those prayers the children had offered up to God, and whose effect could not be long in making itself felt.

"Must I still wait, before I make my determination final?" he asked himself. "Must I wait until God's will manifests itself to me more clearly?"

On the other hand, once on the sidewalk, his religious emotion having abated, the picture of Maud deathly pale in her bed, then the string of grave considerations which in the preceding days had paralyzed his will, came back to him. The sight of his home, like a house totally devastated by fire, passed again before his eyes. He recalled the rigorous command of charity, which bade him first to devote himself to his own family. He persuaded himself, furthermore, that to speak now, after a preparation necessarily so short, would be madness. On the pretext of serving it, might he not be in danger of compromising the schools' cause? Thereupon he immured himself in what he believed was his supreme and final resolution. No, Jules de Lantagnac could not speak; he would not speak.

To Virginia, who was still at his side, and who had suddenly become strangely sad, he could only say:

"How I envy those who will be defending the cause this afternoon!"

"Me too," replied Virginia, "and if it had been God's will, how splendid my father would have appeared to me in that great rôle!"

Then, as if speaking to herself, she added:

"Yet I can't believe that all those children's communions and prayers will not produce something" . . .

During the morning, Lantagnac appeared only briefly at the office, feeling totally out of tune with his legal work. An orator by temperament, the approach of the great debate, even one in which he was not to take part, excited him in much the same way as the sight of the arena sends a thrill through the wrestler. Ideas were bubbling in his brain. In spite of himself, the plan and structure of a speech on the bilingual issue was taking shape in his mind. He was experiencing one of those moments of irrepressible inventiveness, when it seems that all the powers and the fibres of the mind are being brought to the quick by an internal, passionate, almost flaming urge.

Around him, everything seemed to conspire to excite his mind, to add fire to his inspiration. Towards midday, after he had shut himself up in his study and sunk into his armchair, in an effort to escape the strain, his eye chanced to fall on *La tricoteuse endormie,* a painting by Franchère he had recently bought and hung on the wall opposite. The old woman was painted against the encroaching darkness, near her lamp that was empty and dying. Sleep had caught up with her in her rocking-chair. Her head, clad in a white cap, was only half-bent, so normal was it for the old folk of yesteryear to retain the attitude of work even as they slept. Only the sight of her ball of wool, which lay on the ground, unrolled, and of her knitting-needles, one of which had slipped too far over the other, so that they rested on her knees in the form of an elongated cross, made it possible to guess that her eyes were really closed in sleep.

Lantagnac was very fond of this picture. That day, despite himself, he could see in the sleeping figure the whole line of his unknown female forbears, the grandmothers of far-off times, the old Lantagnac and Lamontagne women of the dark periods of the family, then especially his proud, hard-working mother, finally all those women who had mown, spun, and woven so that their children might grow and the common patrimony be increased and strengthened. And suddenly a low, captivating voice seemed to descend from the picture and say to him, in the accents of the deep past:

"Oh child of ours, in your suffering and hesitation, be worthy of us."

Fortunately the bell announcing lunch startled Lantagnac out of this obsession. At table a charming surprise awaited him. Opposite him, roses were displayed in a flower bowl. Maud was there, amazingly recovered from her indisposition. To explain the presence of the roses to her husband, she reminded him that this day was the eve of their twenty-third wedding anniversary. She added:

"And the memory of it, you'll agree, was well worth celebrating."

Virginia bent over the flowers and counted them:

"That's the right number: twenty-three white and twenty-three red."

Lantagnac bent over in his turn, breathing in the scent:

"They carry the whole of spring in their bloom," he said with delight.

"If you remember, Jules," Maud continued, "on the morning of our wedding day, it was white ones like these that you had given me to go to the church. Then, when we left for our honeymoon, it was, like these others again, American beauties that you threw into my arms. Do you remember?"

"Oh" Jules exclaimed, genuinely touched, "you have a simply delightful memory!"

Throughout lunch, Maud remained just as charming. Her joy, slightly too effusive, ill concealed her secret triumph. As Lantagnac was about to get up from the table, the manservant entered and asked:

"Shall I have the car ready for you, Sir?"

"No, if I go out I'll walk."

"In that case," said Maud, "get it for me."

"For you, Maud?" questioned Lantagnac; "aren't you afraid, so soon after your fatigue of last night?"

"No, the doctor approves, and recommends a change."

Lantagnac had been wondering, during the last few days,

whether he would attend the debate. His presence in the House, he felt, would unnecessarily emphasize his silence. Then he had changed his mind. If he could not speak, could he not applaud? He considered that in all honesty he at least owed his friends this evidence of good will. Around two o'clock, therefore, he thought he would set out for the Victoria Museum, where the Commons had been sitting since the February fire. He decided to walk, so as to get some exercise and relax his nerves. He hoped, in addition, that by walking he would deliver himself of the obsessive ideas that were hammering at his brain. The attempt was futile. The arguments, the material he could quote, even the broad, oratorical elaborations none the less continued to take shape and to order themselves in his mind. After he had left Laurier Avenue and entered Elgin Street, magnificent carriages and luxurious automobiles passed by him, carrying gentlemen and particularly ladies in formal attire.

"They're off to be entertained," he thought to himself, as his mind turned to the theatrical passions that would soon grip the parliamentary stage.

He came to the great lawns of the Museum. The building stood at the far side of the empty space; its regular rectangular form, the fake battlements on its roof, and its huge square windows were reminiscent of some big High School. As he passed beside a flowering rose bush, Lantagnac, who had an instinct for elegance, gathered a bud and put it in the lapel of his frock-coat. Then he went in with the crowd of interested people who were surging through the main door. Senator Landry was there, who quickly held out his hand and said to him:

"Thank you for coming."

The MP was already going up the staircase; suddenly, through one of the windows looking on to the large square before the Museum, his attention was drawn to a passing car.

"Isn't that my car?" he thought.

But already the car had become lost in the stream of other vehicles. Lantagnac entered the House. Erect, elegant in the garb that he wore on important occasions, he took his seat on the left of the Speaker, in the space reserved for independents, those who were called the inhabitants of *no man's land.** The House was filled with spectators, as at the solemn moments of parliamentary life. The galleries over-flowed with the fashionable society of the capital. Most of the MP's were already in their seats, chatting in hushed tones. Over the chamber hovered the awesome stillness that is the harbinger of storms to come. Strange currents ran through it, as on stormy summer days, between two claps of thunder, a mysterious breeze, springing up from nowhere, traverses the startled calm of the atmosphere and ruffles the leaves of the trees. From the galleries, opera-glasses, which as they were moved about set up a kind of criss-cross of phosphorescent flashes, peered downwards, scrutinizing the motley crowd of politicians on the rectangular floor. For the benefit of the newcomers, those familiar with the composition of the House outlined its moral geography. Some pointed towards the group of Orangemen, with their clean-shaven, hard faces, the "yellow fellows", as they were called, grumblers by conviction or by habit, who seemed to be stimulated by the hope of a debate in which there would be some fire. Others could pick out by their bored air at the approach of this academic discussion, their sneaky, wheedling manner, their unfailingly secretive way of accosting each other, the profiteers, the great felines of intrigue and finance, who dreamed every evening the dream of the conquistadors, minus their vision of the stars. That day, bowlers and cowboy-style hats were pulled down more firmly over many faces that were trying to accentuate their tough, rancorous expression. But one of the favourites of the gallery, in the front row of the left

*In English in Groulx's original. (Translator's note)

benches, was the leader of the Opposition. His handsome head, with its admirable purity of line — a sculptor's ideal — and his dignified, even rather solemn bearing, reminded one of parliamentarians of a vanished era; he stood out, tasteful in his elegance, a stately anachronism in a House whose ways were becoming more and more democratic. The onlookers also pointed out to each other the author of the resolution, Ernest Lapointe, a giant with an intelligent and good-humoured face, and Paul-Emile Lamarche, radiant with youth and courage, peering over a dossier. But, still more than on the latter two, the eyes of the galleries focused on none other than the member for Russell, whose budding reputation for eloquence and finely modelled head predisposed everyone towards him. Sitting upright in his seat, with his arms crossed, Lantagnac appeared to be waiting in great calm for the curtain to rise. In reality, however, he was finding it hard to tolerate the flashing of the glasses, which appeared to be probing pitilessly into the drama of his life.

The House came to order. In the buzz of talk, a few trifling questions were dispatched with little attention. People were waiting for the great debate. Finally Ernest Lapointe rose. He read his resolution. His text first recalled the guarantees given in respect of religion, customs and language to the peoples who had passed by right of conquest under British rule; it then outlined the grievances of "His Majesty's subjects of French origin in the province of Ontario who are to a large extent deprived as the result of recent legislation, of the privilege of having their children taught in the French language, a privilege which they and their ancestors had always enjoyed since the cession of Canada to the sovereign power of Great Britain"; finally it asked that the House of Commons, "especially in this time of universal sacrifice and anxiety, when all energies should be concentrated on the winning of the war", and, "while fully recognizing the principle of provincial autonomy and the necessity of every child being given a thorough

English education'', respectfully suggest to the Legislature of Ontario ''the wisdom of ensuring that the privilege of children of French parentage to be taught in their mother tongue not be interfered with.''

Discussion began. The speakers on the left showed dignity and courage. After Ernest Lapointe, Sir Wilfrid Laurier addressed the House. In the name of liberalism, of the Anglo-French entente that the war had established in Europe, and of justice, the old statesman entreated Parliament, and particularly the government, to use their influence with the Legislature of Ontario to see that the wrongs done to French Canadians were righted. At times the more eloquent tones of the old parliamentarian, and his franker, more peremptory statements, rang out in the House like a disavowal of the policy of submission too often preached by the same voice. Paul-Emile Lamarche spoke. He did so as a jurist, clearly, methodically, with the strength that independence of character gives to the spoken word. On the government side several spoke in turn, some with barely disguised ill humour, others with a too visible anger, all of them set in their determination to ignore the complaints of the minority, to declare them inopportune, and to let force exert its tyrannical harshness against weakness and right.

The debate appeared to be over. The vote was about to be called. A dramatic shock suddenly passed through the House and the galleries. It was the coup de théâtre which the crowd, anxious for excitement, had been waiting for. The rustle of heads and shoulders moving and turning, rippled briefly through the galleries. On the floor, the parliamentarians themselves were startled in their seats; and all eyes were now focused on the same object. In the back benches on the left, a member had just risen. His voice, with its rich, mellow tone, a little shaky at first, but soon becoming firm and strong, was already resounding through the chamber. What secret influence, what powerful impetus had led the MP for Russell, for he it was, to rise from his seat? He himself, at this moment, would have been hard put to sort out the successive states of mind that had brought him to this decision. At first, his natural integrity had no doubt been distressed by the ambiguous rôle that his silence in the face of those flashing, probing lenses imposed on him. The growing liveliness of the debate had then awakened his eagerness to fight. Finally, while the long list of their grievances and sufferings unfolded, there arose around him, quivering and imperious, the call of his own people, those of his race and province who were the victims of persecution. All these thoughts and feelings had increased in intensity during the speeches of the die-hards of Anglicization. From that moment Lantagnac foresaw that it would be impossible for him to remain riveted to his seat. Could he, the representative of the outraged minority, allow in his presence so many provoking statements to pass without a murmur? Almost at once, his meditations of the day before on Parliament Hill, the precise directives he had brought back from Hull, his reflections of that morning at church had come back to him; and all these glimpses of the truth had stiffened his will, which could not oppose the light of truth itself. Yet, as the speaker remembered, at the last moment something like a mysterious fluid had surged through him; possibly here was one of those extraordinary thrusts of which Father Fabien had spoken, supreme illuminations and impulses from the Holy Spirit, which raise the human will above itself. In a flash the man had found himself on his feet; he had asked to speak, he had begun to speak.

His speech was none the worse for the suddenness of its improvisation. The parliamentary work, which his mind had not been able to eschew, was producing its results. The speech progressed with natural ease, developing its arguments with the regularity and harmony of a classical composition. The speaker relied on the strength of his conscience, and the natural lucidity of his honest mind. He possessed the gifts to please both the House and the galleries. He combined the cold logic and the well-informed, sober style of the English debater with the restrained power of emotion of the lyrical Frenchman, a power which, when handled with conviction, still exercises a strange magnetism on old, blasé parliamentarians.

Lantagnac did not present, like the others before him, another historical account of the Ontario school question, cr expound the rights of bilingualism. The natural elevation of his mind quickly took him to the heights. His speech was an exposé of general ideas, in which his mind soared at ease. Forcefully, reiterating his favorite ideas, he pointed out the danger of the present struggle for the peace of the country and for the continuation of Confederation:

"What object do the persecutors of the French language in Canada seek?" he exclaimed, turning towards the row of ministers. "Do they want, at any price, to rock to its very foundations the edifice so laboriously erected fifty years ago? I shall remind them then of certain obvious realities: along the extensive line separating us from our neighbours to the South, we lack natural frontiers. From one ocean to the other our territories are unified by geography. Frontiers exist only within our country, which they separate into three impenetrable zones. And this is not, alas, the only factor which makes for our division. Western Canada is for free trade; Eastern Canada is protectionist. You, the Anglo-Saxons, are imperialists; we, the sons of Canada, are above all Canadians. How great, then, is the political blindness of this country's politicians who, to all these threats of rupture, deliberately add the fearful clash of religious and national conflicts?"

"Yes," the MP for Russell went on, "the persecutors will perhaps destroy Confederation by killing the faith of my compatriots in federative institutions and by wrecking the principle of the absolute equality of associates, which was the foundation of our political alliance. For, I warn this House, we are too proud a people to consent to indefinite victimization, under a constitution which gave us all equality in this country. Likewise, I warn the ambitious men who perhaps entertain more evil designs against us, to banish fanciful hopes from their minds: we are too strong to succumb to their blows. We are no longer, thanks be to God, the handful of dispossessed that we were in 1760. We are three million strong, undisputed masters of a province of the Dominion that is four times the size of the British Isles. We are the most strongly constituted nationality on the whole North-American continent. Among the human groups established above the forty-fifth parallel, none possesses a more perfect homogeneity than ours; none has adapted better to the atmosphere of the New World; none has more traditions, or more vigorous social institutions. More than a century and a half after being conquered, Quebec remains a national entity whose language and whose soul are as French as in the far-off days of New France. And if amorphous fragments of the German nation or of the poor Polish nationality have been able to triumph over the assimilating power of our formidable neighbours, is it within the capacity of a few thousand persecutors to crush a race whose roots plunge deep into Canadian soil like the maple tree, its immortal symbol?''

Going on from there, and modifying his argument in a way which he knew would give the government and the Ontario persecutors pause for thought, the speaker appealed to the moderate elements and to the Catholic elements of other national groups. To the former, the men of orderly and conservative bent, he portrayed the old Catholic, traditionalist Quebec standing as an insurmountable rampart against antisocial propaganda; he outlined the part that all French communities, across the country, might play in maintaining the Canadian entity, because of their resistance to annexationist tendencies. To the Catholics across Canada, he pointed to the war on bilingual schools as a prologue to sectarian ventures against the Catholic separate schools. In the name of the fraternity of beliefs and misfortunes, he especially implored Irish Catholics to renounce this fratricidal struggle:

"I can well see," he said to them, "what we are both losing in this woeful battle; I do not yet see what our brothers in faith will be able to erect on the ruins of our schools."

For an hour the speaker developed these ideas with an elevation of thought, a perfection of form, and a force of delivery that he had never before attained.

"Often," Emerson has said, "a moment arrives when the spirit of our fathers shines in the clear mirror of our eyes." The spirit of his whole race was alive in the person and in the voice of the member for Russell. Those onlookers who could understand saw the little parliamentary arena expand in size, until it became the battle-field, still open, on which since Sainte-Foy two races and two civilizations have faced each other. Hence the debate took on a solemnity which at times sent a thrill of tragic passion through the House and galleries. At one point, the speaker began to recall the personal suffering of fathers who, because they were unable to give their children an education in conformity with their traditions, felt regretfully that their own sons had become strangers to them. As he uttered these words, Lantagnac involuntarily raised his eyes straight before him, towards the galleries. The last word died in his throat. Suddenly he grew very pale. Why this sudden uneasiness? What had he seen up there? Among the members and in the galleries nothing was suspected: no doubt it was a sudden surge of emotion that constricted the speaker's voice.

Lantagnac sat down amidst almost unanimous applause. Around him, his colleagues congratulated him warmly. And while the galleries were applauding in their own way, by a prolonged buzz of talk impatiently making up for a prolonged silence, Sir Wilfrid Laurier rose from his seat and came to offer the speaker his congratulations:

"My dear Lantagnac," he said to him in a flattering tone, "you are a force to reckon with. Heaven grant that I never have you against me."

In the midst of this triumph, however, Lantagnac remained preoccupied, almost sad. At first, as he resumed his seat, a kind of exaltation had come over him. The deep solemn response of a being stretched to the full extent of its faculties had fired his blood and set his temples throbbing. But this exhilaration was not long in abating. As he took Elgin Street on his way home, an undefinable atmosphere of sadness surrounded him and stayed with him. He suddenly noticed in his buttonhole the rosebud he had gathered on the lawns of the Victoria Museum, and dropped it to the ground. As he passed by an art dealer's shop-front, his eyes fell on a *Victory of Samothrace*. This statue immediately began to haunt his mind. A similar victory seemed to be hovering before him, a wounded, mutilated victory, with death in its fluttering wings. Then, with great anguish, he thought of the reception that awaited him at home. In the gallery, opposite his seat in the House, he could still see the face of the woman whose terrible pallor had so deeply disturbed him at one point in his speech.

That woman was Maud, his own wife.

[X]

When Lantagnac arrived home after a deliberately protracted walk, only Virginia was there to welcome him. The dear child was radiant. She put her arms round her father's neck and clung to him longer than ever before.

"I was there, you know," she cried enthusiastically. "How splendid you were! How impressive you were!"

"Thank you, my dear. Today, however, my strength didn't come from me alone."

Then immediately, in a low voice, he asked:

"What about your mother?"

"She went out with Nellie. When I came home, just now, the maid said: 'Madame has just left; she told me to warn you that she would be late.' "

"I know."

"You noticed her? . . . I guessed so," said Virginia. "And that troubled you deeply."

They were called for dinner. The meal was silent. Neither dared to say any more about the great event of that afternoon, for its impending, almost inevitable consequences oppressed their hearts. Suddenly Lantagnac noticed that the bouquet of roses was no longer on the table.

"Where are the roses that were here at noon?" he asked the maid.

"Madame had them removed a short while ago," the latter replied. "She told me to take them to her room."

This little incident told Lantagnac a great deal about Maud's frame of mind.

"She probably saw my speech this afternoon," he reflected, "as a terrible breach of my word, as a provocative demonstration. And really, what else could she think?"

This interpretation, placed despite himself on his intervention in the debate, had been what had troubled him most when he left the House earlier. During the walk, he had resolutely promised himself that he would confess everything to Maud, with complete frankness. He would tell her that going into the House, and even up to the last moment, his decision had indeed remained the same: to abstain. But he would admit to her that suddenly an irresistible force had raised him from his seat, that his lips had opened, and that he had spoken. Thus he would tell her the exact truth, and he would give his word on it. And that word, he knew, Maud would accept. The absence of his wife forced him to postpone the explanation until the next day.

The next day, indeed, Madame de Lantagnac appeared for lunch, a little tired, very distant, but as always impeccably correct in her manner. Lantagnac vainly tried to bring the conversation round to the delicate subject. With a rare adroitness, Maud was able to turn aside all her husband's allusions to the events of the previous day. Lantagnac concluded that it was better to put off his explanation until later. In the days that followed, Madame remained inviolably entrenched in the same attitude. She maintained it with a constancy and a persistency that were equalled only by her adaptability and her subtlety. So much so that on the home front one could believe the incident was definitely closed and disposed of.

For a few days, Lantagnac enjoyed a sense of serene strength and a more or less unruffled happiness. He felt that he could begin to believe in the fruitfulness of sacrifice, a fruitfulness that Father Fabien had extolled before him in such noble terms. The day after the debate of May eleventh, English opinion was already discussing the Ontario question more calmly, if not more honestly. In Quebec, desire to come to the rescue of the oppressed minority was bringing the parties together. Then Lantagnac recalled the handshake given him by Dan Gallagher, the Irish leader in Ottawa, who had said to him, on leaving the House the other day:

"Thank you, Lantagnac, for drawing attention to those among us who are your friends."

Among his compatriots in Ontario, Lantagnac believed he could observe renewed courage. Each day his mail brought him letters filled with more hope and confidence. Some of them moved him to tears: letters from poor people, badly spelt, written on odd bits of paper, hardly legible, unwittingly sublime. All these happy events brought to his mind an irresistible, absolute certainty: his people would break free and survive. The trials, in the hard fight for liberation, mattered little. His people would experience what he was experiencing himself. Having gradually escaped from the conqueror's grip, having rid itself of everything that it could not assimilate, the French-Canadian people would, as Lantagnac had done, win back the autonomy of its soul, the total control of its existence. And since the dawn of mighty hope was breaking, Lantagnac could see the time approaching when his people, fully emancipated, rulers of a territory which would be a geographic entity, in control of their own moral and material strength, would once again, in full possession of their destiny, take up the ancient dream of the days of New France.

While his life was cheered by these comforting thoughts, each day the peacefulness of his home seemed to increase and become more complete. Only one incident almost revived all his fears momentarily. Just recently he had chanced to pass old

Davis Fletcher on a staircase in the Victoria Museum. Lantagnac had raised his hat to the elderly man; the latter, unheeding and aloof, had gone on his way, his hat firmly on his head, quickening his little scampering steps as fast as he could.

So things went until May twenty-eighth. On that day Lantagnac was at home, working in his study. Virginia suddenly came in, a newspaper in her hand. She was crying.

"Read that," she said.

She pointed to the Ottawa news on the front page, an account of the meeting of the Women's Welfare League. The name of Madame Jules de Lantagnac stood out prominently in the headline. With a worried look, Lantagnac took the paper from his daughter. Virginia saw her father grow pale. The paper reported that at this meeting of the Women's Welfare League, the ladies, very excited by Loyalist passions in wartime, had proposed that *O Canada* be suppressed at the end of their gatherings, and replaced by *God Save the King*. The resolution, proposed by Lady Winston, had been supported by a very large majority, after an enthusiastic speech by Madame de Lantagnac.

Lantagnac dropped the paper on to his lap.

"Virginia," he said firmly, "let us arm ourselves and be prepared for the worst disasters."

His last illusion was vanishing! One could not but see in this news item a retort to the speech of May eleventh. Was not this deliberate intention on his wife's part to oppose her public action to that of her husband, the last step towards their break-up?

In reasoning thus, Lantagnac was only half right. Maud had in reality taken the last step on the day of the debate in the House. Her final decision had been made on the spot, as she sat in her seat in Parliament. Far from seeing in her husband's gesture a lack of loyalty towards her, as Lantagnac had supposed, she saw in it the implacable logic of a loyalty that was too uncompromising. The evil appeared to her irremediable, and it was for that reason that she deemed any explanation with Jules useless and superfluous. On that first day, May eleventh, Maud's decision had been made; from that day she had begun to carry it out.

On the same evening that the paper had published the startling news, she asked her husband to come, not to her room, but to the living room, where she would tell him of her firm decision.

"I have already found a place in Upper Town. I shall leave in four or five days. I want no misunderstanding between us. There must be no scandal before the public. I am leaving quietly. I had warned you of this almost certain outcome. I don't wish to question the motives of your conduct. I ask you not to question my own."

She uttered these brief sentences in a curt tone, with the crease at the corner of the lips and on the forehead that her husband knew all too well as the sign of an unrelenting stubbornness on her part. Lantagnac listened in silence; his expression was grieved, but dignified.

"I know," he said, when she had finished, "I know that your decision is irrevocable. Maud," he went on, looking at her entreatingly, "I want to tell you that I regret this decision deeply . . . deeply."

Somewhat stiffly, she answered:

"It is indeed irrevocable."

"Before your faith, Maud," he dared to ask, "have you thought of your responsibilities?"

"As you have thought of yours, my friend."

Lantagnac shuddered at this bitter remark. Truly disconsolate, he nevertheless hazarded a last question:

"Will you leave me some of my children?"

"I shall respect their freedom," Maud responded icily. "I shall take, you may be sure, only those who choose to follow me."

The conversation ended on this last rejoinder, spoken as Maud rose to leave the room. Lantagnac, who knew her unyielding, terribly imperious character, did nothing to retain her.

Alas! What days lay ahead! The poor husband watched in silence as the preparations for separation were being made. From his study, where he shut himself up as soon as he arrived home, he could hear the noise of furniture being moved out of the rooms and along the corridors, of trunks and packed objects being taken downstairs. Each of these sounds echoed in his heart, like hammer blows on a coffin. One depressing image haunted him and followed him everywhere: that of the dispersal of his children.

"Except for Virginia," he said to himself, "whom shall I have left?"

And would even this last comfort remain to him? The day before Maud was due to leave, as he knew from his beloved child, Virginia entered her father's study. Her red, swollen eyes were evidence enough that she had been crying.

"Father," she said, once she was sitting opposite him, "you have great sorrows. I regret that I'm bringing you another one."

"What is it then, what do you mean, Virginia dear?" asked Lantagnac, growing pale and sadder. "Do you want to leave too?"

"Yes, Father, I want to leave."

"But you're free, perfectly free, my child," said her father, who was at a loss to understand this strange decision.

Virginia went on:

"I want to leave, not with the others, but for always."

Lantagnac gave a cry of distress:

"Ah! Virginia, my only child, I understand: you want to enter the convent! And I shall be alone, all alone! . . ."

And the poor man buried his face in his hands.

"Dear Dad," the child continued, in her most affectionate voice, "do not cry. If I leave, it is so as to be your strength and support even more. You have too much faith for me to need to try to prove it to you. Nearer to God, I shall be closer to you."

She added, as her father raised his head:

"I also want to be associated with your work of reparation and conquest. After you, as you are sadly aware, there will be Lantagnacs who will fight the traditions of their forbears. For myself, I want to teach the language of my forbears and my father; I want to extend its use so that the action of the others may be neutralized. There will also be, as you fear, Lantagnacs whom mixed marriages will expose to the loss of their faith: Nellie has a Protestant fiancé, Wolfred a Protestant fiancée. I hope that God will accept my sacrifice on their behalf."

"Wonderful child!" cried Lantagnac, drawing her towards him. "May you be blessed, Virginia; go where God calls you. Your poor father will tend his incurable wounds as best he can."

"God himself will tend them for you," replied the young girl, with an inspired air.

Then, standing before him:

"Now I have another sacrifice to request of you."

"What?" asked Lantagnac immediately, once more alarmed.

"Tomorrow, you will allow me to leave with Mother. Whatever impression she gives, her departure will be terribly hard for her, I know. Allow me to stay with her for a few days. After that, I promise, I'll return. We'll go to Saint-Michel and stay together for a few weeks before my last good-bye. Will you?"

"Very well, Virginia, you shall go; one sacrifice more or less is of no further consequence."

"Thank you, dearest Father," said the young girl, kissing him on the forehead, and uttering a further word of hope:

"Who knows whether God will not permit me to rebuild the future between you and Mother?"

Left alone, the luckless father felt the need to summon up all his energy in order not to give way. Instinctively he lifted his eyes to the bronze crucifix hanging above his desk. And it was in a voice filled with all the urgent entreaty of his soul that he cried out:

"Oh God! Oh God! has the iron wedge not yet finished its work? Will it not fall at last? . . ."

Exhausted, and drained by so much mental suffering that had accumulated in the last few months, he was seized by a sudden dread: where would he find the strength to face the good-byes of Maud and Nellie? In his weakness, he feared this tragic moment above all else.

Providence took care of it. The next day, when Lantagnac returned home, at dinner time, he immediately noticed the heavy silence in the house: it was deserted. Only the manservant and two maids remained. Maud, who had dreaded the final moment still more than her husband, had decided to leave while the head of the household was away. He, far from feeling relieved, was now affected by a heart-rending sadness at this hasty departure, this separation without a word of farewell. That evening he took his seat at the table, but could not eat. His heart heavy with grief, he roamed all over the house, wandering from room to room, from floor to floor, as if looking for the absent ones. Cautiously, with a sense of terror, he pushed open the door of Maud's room. A strange smell, the smell of an abandoned house, assailed him. The room was empty. On the walls, the paper was streaked with white lines left by the edges of picture frames and pieces of furniture. Here and there on the floor, the dust had collected in little fleecy tufts. One odd but poignant little detail: in the middle of the floor, forgotten during the move, lay a castor from the leg of a bed. Lantagnac closed the door again, as if driven out by the air of a funeral vault. From there he went into Nellie's room. The same emptiness and the same atmosphere greeted him. In William's room a book had been left, apparently forgotten, on a table: *L'Avenir du peuple canadien-français* by

Edmond de Nevers, a volume that Lantagnac had lent to his son during the Christmas holidays. The pages were uncut; on the first blank page was written insolently, in William's hand: "Rule Britannia for ever!" In Wolfred's room, as in Virginia's, nothing was disturbed.

Lantagnac went down to his study. Mechanically he gathered before him the pictures of Maud, Nellie, Wolfred, Virginia, and William; he put his head in his hands and let his heart overflow. He wept copiously in the silence which, for the first time, revealed to him his frightful solitude. Then the catastrophe forced him brutally to re-examine his responsibilities. Moreover, a pitiless voice which he felt rising from his conscience and his misery said to him:

"For your misfortune, begin by blaming yourself. It was you who committed the first mistake twenty-three years ago. By this marriage which made you so proud, you constructed a homestead of ill-matched, fragile materials. Why complain that the iron wedge has burst everything asunder?"

For a long time Lantagnac allowed these feelings and thoughts to seethe in his mind. Now and again he thought his life and his courage were broken for ever. Yet, each time his eyes turned towards Virginia's photograph, a secret strength entered into him. Was it the sacrifice of this noble child, her mysterious power, which were already beginning to operate? He repeated to himself the last words she had spoken to him, the memory of which was as soothing as balm.

Then, as he needed to cling to the slightest hope, he began to think about Wolfred. A telegram was on his table announcing the student's arrival by the evening train.

"In an hour at the most," he said to himself, "Wolfred will be here. What is he coming to tell me? In which direction will he go, I wonder?"

He had learned from Virginia that William had written to his mother, asking to have all his belongings taken to her new home. Wolfred had written nothing. What decision would the elder boy make? Lantagnac recalled at that moment the letter from Wolfred, which he had received two months earlier. At the time, he had read it somewhat distractedly; but he had not forgotten the strange memory it had left with him! He opened a drawer in his desk, and began rereading the small sheets of paper, covered with a fine, closely written script. Wolfred was confiding to his father his first impressions of the Montreal environment. As always, the student had written with his touch of dry satire, and a sort of verbal truculence that sometimes frightened Lantagnac:

Ah, my dear Father, he wrote, so I must tell you about your dear Montreal. In my naïvety, which was as juvenile as it was virginal, and I admit at least as virginal as it was juvenile, I had looked forward to discovering a French town here, something like a replica of Bordeaux or Lyon, in short the third French city in the world after Paris! I was curious to observe an original physiognomy, customs unknown to me, which would provide a rest from the sham and dullness of my English environment. To get straight to the point, I'll tell you that I was tingling with excitement, the way Rica and Usbeck were when they arrived in Paris. Ah yes, poor me, I should have played blasé right away, like a fossil or a politician, and thus given myself the air of a young 'Regency' buck! Immediately upon my arrival, last fall, I started to explore Montreal. What did I see? What did I discover, except perfect imitations of the most authentic American emporia? So that's what it was! . . . I moved about and looked around. Every hundred yards or so, I was dumbfounded, as an Ontarian, to come across a pure Norman name, invariably coupled to a sign — sometimes in the French language. One might almost have thought one was in Québec city. And what of this French-Canadian society of yours! Recently, I have entered some of those social circles, which I had been told were as closed as an Indian caste. My name, but more than anything else my English education, acted as a passport. Well, here again, will you believe me? All those well-established, affected snobs, to whom I served up my best French, often answered me only in their bad English. Alas! must I tell you, Father, you, one of the leaders of resistance in Ontario? The children of the Bossangers, the Frontenacs, the Giboyers, the Rougemonts — all people of Quebec — attend mostly English schools and prefer to speak among themselves the language of the 'superior race'. A little girl of the Gaudarville family spoke to me in English with a perfect cockney accent. Yes, one makes that distinction here. Furthermore, these smart chatterers who regard Westmount as their Sinai smoke their cigarettes at the 'five o'clock teas' with more elegance even than our English ladies. Ah! weep, mothers of our country, weep! Besides, this bourgeois nobility makes no secret of the fact that it harbours the most natural contempt for its race. Ready enough to cry 'Long live France!' in a voice quavering with ecstasy, you will never hear it say 'Long live Canada!' The mere chance of having dined at the Mount Royal Club, with some Anglo-Saxon financier or other, is enough to send a person off exclaiming admiringly: 'Ah, the English, my dear, the English, what a superior breed of men!'

The letter continued in this vein. With the same thoroughly ungracious impertinence, Wolfred described "a number of coteries of impudent young puppies, would-be academies, which are no more than second-rate cafés of a fake Paris." He spoke of "literary works produced by callow youths whose specialty is spineless literature, their sublime ambition being to uproot themselves, to empty their work so completely of any substantial content that it will retain no vestige of their race, their motherland, or their faith. The saddest thing is not that they consider themselves prophets of a new art, but that they are incapable of perceiving that people like themselves have never been anything but a fungus on decadent literatures, and too childish to realize that a literature which loses itself in subtleties in its beginnings is born diseased rather than healthy . . .''. ''Besides,'' Wolfred's letter concluded, ''these ferocious aesthetes also despise their compatriots, hate their barbarous homeland, and under the pretext of humanizing themselves are denationalizing themselves.''

Lantagnac dropped the small sheets on his desk. Reading this letter only increased his sadness. Granted, before closing, Wolfred promised his father a further missive and other impressions. But the tone of this first letter was so bitter and so disheartened!

''Oh, how far poor Wolfred still is from his own people,'' he reflected. ''He has seen nothing of the real inner life of Quebec; nothing either, in Montreal itself, of the admirable effort, pursued with a crusading ardour, to restore to the city its French character, not so much in its soul, which has always remained French, but in its external appearance. Poor boy! He has only seen the surface. But can he, with the eyes of a stranger, see anything else?''

Lantagnac picked up the letter again. His eyes suddenly fell on the signature. Was it absent-mindedness or deliberate intention on his son's part? Lantagnac looked a second time. He was not mistaken. The letter was indeed signed, not with his son's first name, Wolfred, but with his second: André, André de Lantagnac. This novelty made the father ask himself again, but with greater anxiety, the same question as earlier: what was happening to his elder boy? What was the meaning of this French Christian name, appended for the first time at the bottom of one of his letters?

Some twenty minutes later the front doorbell rang vigorously; quick steps were heard on the staircase; a young man appeared at the door of Lantagnac's study: it was Wolfred.

"I know everything," he said as he came in. "I know everything. And that's why I've come. Ah, Father! Ah, poor Mother!"

"Ah, poor Wolfred!" his father replied, giving his hands a long affectionate clasp. "Thank you for coming."

"And you are left alone?"

"Absolutely alone up till now."

"But Virginia?"

"She is going to enter the convent. Meanwhile, she has asked permission to stay with her mother, for a few days."

"Ah, Father, what a misfortune for you and us all!"

"Yes," replied Lantagnac, very downcast; "after this separation, worse for me than death, I am only left — as Father Fabien says — with one fiancée, perhaps: the cause to which I shall henceforth devote my life."

Then, looking his son in the eyes, he added immediately, in a tone of pathetic entreaty:

"And I have one hope remaining on this earth, one only: that I will see my elder son, you, Wolfred, return to me with a soul that has become French again."

Wolfred lowered his eyes a moment, then raised them again; there was a passionate gleam in them as he said:

"Well, Father, let's celebrate this return together. It has already happened."

Lantagnac opened his arms.

"No, Father," said Wolfred, "not like that, but on my knees. And give me your blessing, the blessing of New Year's day that I didn't have the courage to ask for. It is by that means that I want to return to the tradition of my forbears."

Lantagnac, unable to utter a word, put his hands on his son's head.

Wolfred got up again. His father asked him to sit opposite him. Then, having recovered a little from his intense emotion,

Lantagnac began to ply his son with questions, begging him to describe his conversion in detail.

"How did you come to it?" he asked him. "Your letter this winter was hardly encouraging, you know. Speak, my son."

Wolfred was only too anxious to speak.

"Indeed," he said, "that letter must have brought you some very pessimistic impressions. However, as I recall, I promised you some of a different kind. It is those impressions that have brought me back."

"Tell me, Wolfred, tell me everything," insisted Lantagnac, rapidly recovering from his dejection.

"Well, to be frank with you," began Wolfred, "I believe what triggered it was my first contact with the land of Quebec. Do you remember our first evening at the cottage, on Lake MacGregor, and our trip on the lake? All at once, the land spoke to me with a beauty and charm all its own, and the lesson was not lost. Once begun, my evolution was nurtured by very thorough readings of carefully chosen French works, which soon restored in me a sense of coherence and balance. My progress became a perceptible reality to me, I would even say a joy. This was already, I think, the great turning point. You may not believe it, but the defections among our own people gave me the second push. At the sight of those men and women who had ostentatiously taken on a mentality that wasn't their own, I felt that an iron hand had descended on the soul of my people. My young pride revolted. I was reading our history at the time. In it I discovered, every day, the old soil in which my spirit had its natural roots. Beside those deserters, few in number, I could see the others, those who have resisted, and who go on resisting and who carry a whole people with them. Shall I admit it? The sight of that little group of Frenchmen, surrounded by a hundred or so millions of Anglo-Saxons, but magnificently persistent in not giving in, the sight of that American Alsace-Lorraine, more alone and more forgotten that the other one, but no less enduring, no less faithful to itself for a period of one hundred and sixty-six years, the sight of a people that places above all material ambitions the pride of its culture and the worth of its soul, that is a sight which I assure you I found to be of stirring beauty, superior to anything that the other civilization had shown me until then. I noted also to my great joy, that if the Anglo-Saxons subjugate a few odd groups pretty well everywhere as they do here, with their money and their customs, they subjugate no one by their literature and their arts. At about the same time, I began to move in other circles than those of the Anglicized bourgeoisie . . .''

"Tell me," interrupted Lantagnac, "didn't you judge that bourgeoisie rather too severely?"

"I'll say yes to that," conceded Wolfred. "Anyway, apart from the snobs and social climbers, it counts for little, you know, either in terms of numbers or credit . . . So, my best piece of luck around that time was to make my way into the homes of some of my teachers, the leaders of the young generation. There I discovered what you often called in front of me, although I didn't understand you too well, Franco-Latin culture. Grace, effortless knowledge naturally acquired, true culture, poise, spiritual refinement were revealed to me. It was proved to me that to remain French in this country is a sign of sensitivity as well as nobility of mind. Consequently, I can say that from that moment on the Anglo-Saxon mirage was almost at an end for me. Like you, I respect my mother's race; but I no longer exalt it above another."

Wolfred had spoken animatedly, with infectious enthusiasm. His father had listened to him, interrupting him only once, gripped by interest in his speech and the tone of these youthful words, ardent and beautiful as those of a future orator. At this point, however, Lantagnac, consumed with a desire to find out everything, could not restrain his curiosity:

"Almost at an end, you say? Almost? . . . So other causes influenced you?"

"The other day," Wolfred went on, with deeper feeling, "I followed a pilgrimage of *L'Action Française* from Montreal to the Long-Sault, Dollard's country. You remember the picture of Dollard by Delfosse that you once hung on the wall of my room. At that time I didn't pay much attention to it. However, as time passed and my evolution progressed, that mighty trumpeter sounding the charge haunted my thoughts: an imperious model, an irresistible leader of men. The other day, as you no doubt read in the papers, a group of patriots went to the actual scene of the combat of 1660, to inaugurate a monument to the sublime hero of New France. I followed them. There I found the kind of site I love, one that would have pleased Barrès: a secluded, enclosed place, made for meditation, the background topped by a *'colline inspirée'*, then falling away towards the majestic surface of a flowing river. Absorbed in my meditations, I wandered away from the crowd. I climbed the high slopes. I went and sat on the grass, opposite the Long-Sault, under the old, shady trees. With the murmur of the waters, some of the more ringing phrases of the speakers came to me on the wind. Under the age-old trees, this eloquence sounded in my ears like the snapping cloth of a flag. Then I took out of my briefcase your speech of May eleventh, which I had read in the copy of Hansard you had sent to me. Father, how can I describe to you the effect of your words on my young mind in that place, in the presence of those memories from the past! I knew the heart-rending drama that was being played out here. I had to choose between two courses. Well, your word was the stronger, because in me, at the Long-Sault, its resonance was the same as that of history. Instinctively I got up; trembling, I stretched out my arm towards the monument of the hero. There, I tell you, yes, there, I swore it aloud; I shall be on my father's side, French like him and my ancestors, wholly and enthusiastically French!"

The young man had risen, his face lit as by a flame, his eyes filled with emotion, his whole person transfigured by his lyricism. The father looked at his son. An exalted pride welled up in him. For a moment he hesitated. A question came to his lips. Would he dare ask it? Was it really the time? Yes, after all, it was. At that moment he needed to feel reassured, fully and absolutely reassured.

"Wolfred, my son, forgive me, but French you said? Have you considered everything? Have you considered your fiancée, my poor fellow?"

The young man placed his hand on his heart:

"My fiancée? Since yesterday, my fiancée is none other than yours."

Lantagnac opened his arms once more. His son threw himself into them, choking back a sob. For a long time they clung to each other, in the grip of a supreme emotion in which was concentrated all that is most tragic in human life.

"Ah, Wolfred!" said Lantagnac, straightening himself up again.

"Ah, Father," his son corrected him gently, "don't call me anything but André. For you and for everyone, from now on, I am André de Lantagnac."

THE CARLETON LIBRARY SERIES

1. LORD DURHAM'S REPORT, edited and with an Introduction by Gerald M. Craig
2. THE CONFEDERATION DEBATES IN THE PROVINCE OF CANADA, 1865, edited and with an Introduction by P.B. Waite
3. LAURIER: A STUDY IN CANADIAN POLITICS, by J.W. Dafoe, with an Introduction by Murray S. Donnelly
4. CHAMPLAIN: THE LIFE OF FORTITUDE, by Morris Bishop, with a new Introduction by the author
5. THE ROWELL-SIROIS REPORT, *Book I*, edited and with an Introduction by Donald V. Smiley
6. THE UNREFORMED SENATE OF CANADA, by Robert A. MacKay, revised and with an Introduction by the author
7. THE JESUIT RELATIONS AND ALLIED DOCUMENTS: A SELECTION, edited and with an Introduction by S.R. Mealing
8. LORD DURHAM'S MISSION TO CANADA, by Chester New, edited and with an Introduction by H.W. McCready
9. THE RECIPROCITY TREATY OF 1854, by Donald C. Masters, with a new Introduction by the author
10. POLITICAL UNREST IN UPPER CANADA, 1815-1836, by Aileen Dunham, with an Introduction by A.L. Burt
11. A HISTORY OF TRANSPORTATION IN CANADA, *Volume I*, by G.P. deT. Glazebrook, with a new Introduction by the author
12. A HISTORY OF TRANSPORTATION IN CANADA, *Volume II*, by G.P. deT. Glazebrook
13. THE ECONOMIC BACKGROUND OF DOMINION-PROVINCIAL RELATIONS, by W.A. Mackintosh, with an Introduction by J.H. Dales
14. THE FRENCH-CANADIAN OUTLOOK, by Mason Wade, with a new Introduction by the author
15. THE WESTERN INTERIOR OF CANADA: A RECORD OF GEOGRAPHICAL DISCOVERY, 1612-1917, edited and with an Introduction by John Warkentin
16. THE COURTS AND THE CANADIAN CONSTITUTION, edited and with an Introduction by W.R. Lederman
17. MONEY AND BANKING IN CANADA, edited and with an Introduction by E.P. Neufeld
18. FRENCH-CANADIAN SOCIETY, *Volume I*, edited and with an Introduction by Marcel Rioux and Yves Martin
19. THE CANADIAN COMMERCIAL REVOLUTION, 1845-1851, by Gilbert N. Tucker, edited and with an Introduction by Hugh G.J. Aitken
20. JOSEPH HOWE: VOICE OF NOVA SCOTIA, edited and with an Introduction by J. Murray Beck

21. LIFE AND LETTERS OF SIR WILFRID LAURIER, *Volume I*, by Oscar Douglas Skelton, edited and with an Introduction by David M.L. Farr
22. LIFE AND LETTERS OF SIR WILFRID LAURIER, *Volume II*, by Oscar Douglas Skelton, edited by David M.L. Farr
23. LEADING CONSTITUTIONAL DECISIONS, edited and with an Introduction by Peter H. Russell
24. FRONTENAC, THE COURTIER GOVERNOR, by W.J. Eccles
25. INDIANS OF THE NORTH PACIFIC COAST, edited and with an Introduction by Tom McFeat
26. LIFE AND TIMES OF SIR ALEXANDER TILLOCH GALT, by Oscar Douglas Skelton, edited and with an Introduction by Guy MacLean
27. A HISTORY OF CANADIAN EXTERNAL RELATIONS, *Volume I*, by G.P. deT. Glazebrook, revised by the author
28. A HISTORY OF CANADIAN EXTERNAL RELATIONS, *Volume II*, by G.P. deT. Glazebrook, revised and with a Bibliographical Essay by the author
29. THE RACE QUESTION IN CANADA, by André Siegfried, edited and with an Introduction by Frank H. Underhill
30. NORTH ATLANTIC TRIANGLE, by John Bartlett Brebner, with an Introduction by Donald G. Creighton
31. APPROACHES TO CANADIAN ECONOMIC HISTORY, edited and with an Introduction by W.T. Easterbrook and M.H. Watkins
32. CANADIAN SOCIAL STRUCTURE: A STATISTICAL PROFILE, edited and with an Introduction and Commentary by John Porter
33. CHURCH AND STATE IN CANADA, 1627-1867: BASIC DOCUMENTS, edited and with an Introduction by John S. Moir
34. WESTERN ONTARIO AND THE AMERICAN FRONTIER, by Fred Landon, with a new Introduction by the author
35. HISTORICAL ESSAYS ON THE ATLANTIC PROVINCES, edited and with an Introduction by G.A. Rawlyk
36. A HISTORY OF JOURNALISM IN CANADA, by W.H. Kesterton, with an Introduction by Wilfrid Eggleston
37. THE OLD PROVINCE OF QUEBEC, *Volume I*, by A.L. Burt, with an Introduction by Hilda Neatby
38. THE OLD PROVINCE OF QUEBEC, *Volume II*, by A.L. Burt
39. GROWTH AND THE CANADIAN ECONOMY, edited and with an Introduction by T.N. Brewis
40. DOCUMENTS ON THE CONFEDERATION OF BRITISH NORTH AMERICA, edited and with an Introduction by G.P. Browne
41. ESKIMO OF THE CANADIAN ARCTIC, edited and with an Introduction by Victor F. Valentine and Frank G. Vallee
42. THE COLONIAL REFORMERS AND CANADA, 1830-1849, edited and with an Introduction by Peter Burroughs
43. A NARRATIVE, by Sir Francis Bond Head, edited and with an Introduction by S.F. Wise

44. JOHN STRACHAN: DOCUMENTS AND OPINIONS, edited and with an Introduction by J.L.H. Henderson
45. THE NEUTRAL YANKEES OF NOVA SCOTIA, by J.B. Brebner, with an Introduction by W.S. MacNutt
46. ROBERT LAIRD BORDEN: HIS MEMOIRS, *Volume I*, edited and with an Introduction by Heath Macquarrie
47. ROBERT LAIRD BORDEN: HIS MEMOIRS, *Volume II*, edited by Heath Macquarrie
48. THE CANADIAN MUNICIPAL SYSTEM: ESSAYS ON THE IMPROVEMENT OF LOCAL GOVERNMENT, by D.C. Rowat
49. THE BETTER PART OF VALOUR: ESSAYS ON CANADIAN DIPLOMACY, by John W. Holmes
50. LAMENT FOR A NATION: THE DEFEAT OF CANADIAN NATIONALISM, by George Grant, with a new Introduction by the author
51. CANADIAN FOREIGN POLICY, 1945-1954, by R.A. MacKay, edited and with an Introduction by the author
52. MONCK: LETTERS AND JOURNALS, edited and with an Introduction by W.L. Morton
53. HISTORICAL ESSAYS ON THE PRAIRIE PROVINCES, edited and with an Introduction by Donald Swainson
54. THE CANADIAN ECONOMY IN THE GREAT DEPRESSION, by A.E. Safarian
55. CANADA'S CHANGING NORTH, edited and with an Introduction by William C. Wonders
56. THE DEVELOPMENT OF CANADA'S STAPLES, 1867-1939, edited and with an Introductory comment by Kevin H. Burley
57. URBAN DEVELOPMENT IN SOUTH-CENTRAL ONTARIO, by Jacob Spelt
58. CULTURE AND NATIONALITY: ESSAYS BY A.G. BAILEY, by Alfred Goldsworthy Bailey
59. COMMUNITY IN CRISIS: FRENCH-CANADIAN NATIONALISM IN PERSPECTIVE, by Richard Jones, with a new Introduction by the author
60. PERSPECTIVES ON THE NORTH AMERICAN INDIANS, edited and with an Introduction by Mark Nagler
61. LANGUAGES IN CONFLICT, by Richard J. Joy, with a Preface by Frank G. Vallee
62. THE LAST FORTY YEARS: THE UNION OF 1841 TO CONFEDERATION, by J.C. Dent, abridged and with an Introduction by Donald Swainson
63. LAURIER AND A LIBERAL QUEBEC: A STUDY IN POLITICAL MANAGEMENT, by H. Blair Neatby, edited and with an Introduction by Richard T. Clippingdale
64. THE TREMBLAY REPORT, edited and with an Introduction by David Kwavnick

65. CULTURAL ECOLOGY: READINGS ON THE CANADIAN INDIANS AND ESKIMOS, edited and with an Introduction by Bruce Cox
66. RECOLLECTIONS OF THE ON TO OTTAWA TREK, by Ronald Liversedge, with Documents Relating to the Vancouver Strike and the On to Ottawa Trek, edited and with an Introduction by Victor Hoar
67. THE OMBUDSMAN PLAN: ESSAYS ON THE WORLDWIDE SPREAD OF AN IDEA, by Donald C. Rowat
68. NATURAL RESOURCES: THE ECONOMICS OF CONSERVATION, by Anthony Scott
69. "DOMINION LANDS" POLICY, by Chester Martin, edited and with an Introduction by Lewis H. Thomas
70. RENEGADE IN POWER: THE DIEFENBAKER YEARS, by Peter C. Newman, with an Introduction by Denis Smith
71. CUTHBERT GRANT OF GRANTOWN, by Margaret A. MacLeod and W.L. Morton
72. THE NATIVE PEOPLES OF ATLANTIC CANADA: A READER IN REGIONAL ETHNIC RELATIONS, by H.F. McGee
73. FREEDOM AND ORDER/COLLECTED ESSAYS, by Eugene Forsey, with an Introduction by Donald Creighton
74. THE CRISIS OF QUEBEC, 1914-1918, by Elizabeth Armstrong, with an Introduction by Joseph Levitt
75. STATISTICAL ACCOUNT OF UPPER CANADA, by Robert Gourlay, abridged, and with an Introduction by S.R. Mealing
76. THE ADVENTURES AND SUFFERINGS OF JOHN JEWITT CAPTIVE AMONG THE NOOTKA, edited and with an Introduction by Derek G. Smith
77. CAPITAL FORMATION IN CANADA, 1896-1930, by Kenneth Buckley, with an Introduction by M. Urquhart
78. BEYOND THE ATLANTIC ROAR: A STUDY OF THE NOVA SCOTIA SCOTS, by D. Campbell and R.A. MacLean
79. CONSOCIATIONAL DEMOCRACY, by K.D. McRae
80. PHILIPPE DE RIGAUD DE VAUDREUIL, GOVERNOR OF NEW FRANCE 1703-1725, by Yves Zoltvany
81. CANADIAN-AMERICAN SUMMIT DIPLOMACY, 1923-1973, by Roger Frank Swanson
82. HISTORICAL ESSAYS ON UPPER CANADA, by J.K. Johnson
83. THE CANADIAN BILL OF RIGHTS, by Walter Surma Tarnopolsky
84. SOCIALIZATION AND VALUES IN CONTEMPORARY CANADA, *Volume I, Political Socialization*, edited by Elia Zureik and Robert M. Pike
85. SOCIALIZATION AND VALUES IN CONTEMPORARY CANADA, *Volume II: Socialization, Social Stratification and Ethnicity*, edited by Robert M. Pike and Elia Zureik
86. CANADA'S BALANCE OF INTERNATIONAL INDEBTEDNESS, 1910-1913, by Jacob Viner

87. CANADIAN INDIANS AND THE LAW: SELECTED DOCUMENTS, 1663-1972, edited by Derek G. Smith
88. LIVING AND LEARNING IN THE FREE SCHOOL, by Mark Novak
89. THE CANADIAN CORPORATE ELITE: AN ANALYSIS OF ECONOMIC POWER, by Wallace Clement
90. MAN'S IMPACT ON THE WESTERN CANADIAN LANDSCAPE, by J.G. Nelson
91. PERSPECTIVES ON LANDSCAPE AND SETTLEMENT IN NINETEENTH CENTURY ONTARIO, edited by J. David Wood
92. MINORITY MEN IN A MAJORITY SETTING, by Christopher Beattie
93. CANADIAN-AMERICAN INDUSTRY, by Herbert Marshall, Frank Southard, Jr., and Kenneth W. Taylor
94. CAPITAL PUNISHMENT IN CANADA, by David Chandler
95. POLITICAL CORRUPTION IN CANADA: CASES, CAUSES, CURES, edited by Kenneth Gibbons and Donald C. Rowat
96. HISTORICAL ESSAYS ON BRITISH COLUMBIA, edited by J. Friesen and H.K. Ralston
97. THE FROG LAKE "MASSACRE": PERSONAL PERSPECTIVES ON ETHNIC CONFLICT, edited and with an Introduction by Stuart Hughes
98. CANADA: A MIDDLE-AGED POWER, by John W. Holmes
99. EIGHTEENTH CENTURY NEWFOUNDLAND: A GEOGRAPHIC PERSPECTIVE, by C. Grant Head
100. THE LAW AND THE PRESS IN CANADA, by Wilfrid H. Kesterton
101. THE AGRICULTURAL ECONOMY OF MANITOBA HUTTERITE COLONIES, by John Ryan
102. THE FRONTIER AND CANADIAN LETTERS, by Wilfrid Eggleston, with an Introduction by Douglas Spettigue
103. CANADIAN FOREIGN POLICY, 1955-1965, by A.E. Blanchette
104. A CRITICAL SPIRIT: THE THOUGHT OF WILLIAM DAWSON LESUEUR, edited and with an Introduction by A.B. McKillop
105. CHOOSING CANADA'S CAPITAL: JEALOUSY AND FRICTION IN THE 19TH CENTURY, by David B. Knight
106. THE CANADIAN QUANDARY: ECONOMIC PROBLEMS AND POLICIES, by Harry G. Johnson
107. KEYNESIAN ECONOMICS, by Mabel F. Timlin, with a biographical note by A.E. Safarian and a Foreword by L. Tarshis
108. THE DOUKHOBORS, by George Woodcock and Ivan Avakumovic
109. THE CANADIAN CITY: ESSAYS IN URBAN HISTORY, edited by Gilbert A. Stelter and Alan F.J. Artibise
110. DOES MONEY MATTER? by John Porter, Marion R. Porter and Bernard Blishen
111. WILLIAM LYON MACKENZIE: A REINTERPRETATION by William Dawson LeSueur, edited and with introduction by A.B. McKillop
112. THE DISTEMPER OF OUR TIMES, by Peter C. Newman
113. THE CANADIAN ECONOMY AND DISARMAMENT, by Gideon Rosenbluth

THE CARLETON LIBRARY SERIES

114. THE FARMERS IN POLITICS, by William Irvine with Introduction by R. Whitaker

115. THE BOUNDARIES OF THE CANADIAN CONFEDERATION, by Norman Nicholson

116. EACH FOR ALL, by Ian Macpherson

117. CANADIAN CONFEDERATION: A DECISION-MAKING ANALYSIS, by W.L. White, R.H. Wagenberg, R.C. Nelson and W.C. Soderlund

118. CANADIAN FOREIGN POLICY 1966-1976, edited by Arthur E. Blanchette

119. THE USABLE URBAN PAST, edited by Alan J. Artibise and Gilbert A. Stelter

120. ECONOMIC AND SOCIAL HISTORY OF QUEBEC, 1760-1850, by Fernand Ouellet

122. LAST OF THE FREE ENTERPRISERS: THE OILMEN OF CALGARY, by J.D. House

123. CONTEXTS OF CANADA'S PAST. Essays of W.L. Morton, edited by A.B. McKillop.

124. THE REDISTRIBUTION OF INCOME IN CANADA, by W. Irwin Gillespie

125. SHAPING THE URBAN LANDSCAPE: ASPECTS OF THE CANADIAN CITY-BUILDING PROCESS, edited by Gilbert A. Stelter and Alan F.J. Artibise

126. RECREATIONAL LAND USE: PERSPECTIVES ON ITS EVOLUTION IN CANADA, edited by G. Wall and J. Marsh

127. FEAR'S FOLLY (LES DEMI-CIVILISES) by Jean-Charles Harvey. Translated by John Glassco, edited by John O'Connor

128. THE ENTERPRISES OF ROBERT HAMILTON: Wealth and Influence in Early Upper Canada, 1776-1812, by Bruce G. Wilson

129. THE SOCIOLOGY OF WORK: Papers in Honour of Oswald Hall, edited by Audrey Wipper

130. CULTURAL DIVERSITY AND SCHOOLING IN CANADA: edited by John R. Mallea & Jonathan C. Young

131. ABORIGINAL PEOPLE AND THE LAW, edited by Bradford W. Morse